SUMMER SUN, WINTER DREAMS

The holiday in Spain was so important for Kathryn and her young daughter, Deborah, but, unfortunately, it got off to a bad start. Then, thanks to the intervention of Rafael Delvega, it turned into the holiday Kathryn had dreamed of. Rafael Delvega was so thoughtful and attractive that Kathryn began to have other dreams too, dreams which died painfully when she suddenly had to face what kind of man he really was. By then it was too late and the heartbreak began.

Books by Joanna Logan
in the Linford Romance Library:

WINTER HARVEST

JOANNA LOGAN

SUMMER SUN, WINTER DREAMS

Complete and Unabridged

LINFORD
Leicester

First published in Great Britain in 1990 by
Robert Hale Limited
London

First Linford Edition
published 1997
by arrangement with
Robert Hale Limited
London

British Library CIP Data

Logan, Joanna
    Summer sun, winter dreams.—Large print ed.—
Linford romance library
    1. Love stories
    2. Large type books
    I. Title
823.9'14 [F]

ISBN 0–7089–5175–9

Published by
F. A. Thorpe (Publishing) Ltd.
Anstey, Leicestershire

Set by Words & Graphics Ltd.
Anstey, Leicestershire
Printed and bound in Great Britain by
T. J. International Ltd., Padstow, Cornwall

This book is printed on acid-free paper

1

"**A**RE you saying we can't stay at this hotel?"

At this stage people who knew Kathryn Morris well would have recognised her expression and paused to consider their next words carefully.

Lacking such knowledge the receptionist went on, "That is correct, Señora. You will go to another hotel. A room is reserved for you and the little one."

The 'little one' looked bewildered by the conversation being carried on over her head.

"And where is this hotel?" Kathryn asked in a deceptively level tone.

"In a small village twenty-five kilometres inland," the receptionist replied. "A coach will take you."

Kathryn did some quick arithmetic. "That's fifteen miles! How do we get to the beach?"

"There is a local taxi," the man answered. "Now, Señora, the coach waits outside for you."

"It can wait," Kathryn snapped. "I'm not making a thirty-mile round trip to the beach every day." She turned to the courier standing beside her. "What do you propose to do about this?"

The young woman was apologetic. "Unfortunately overbooking does occur from time to time. Accommodation has been reserved and, in my experience, it's usually superior to the original." She smiled, hoping to have placated the irate woman.

Kathryn was not to be placated. "I'm not going," she flatly stated. "I booked into the Christoval and here I want to stay." Her blue eyes turned once more to the receptionist. "Do you understand?"

The man shrugged. "Nothing can be done. Please go out to the coach."

After the disasters of the past year his dismissive attitude towards the ruination of their holiday was the final straw. Kathryn slammed her handbag on the counter. "Get the manager. I want this sorted out properly."

"Mrs Morris," the courier put in, "if the hotel has no room, it has no room?"

"True," Kathryn agreed, "but the least they can do is provide free transport so my daughter can have the seaside holiday she's been looking forward to."

Paying for the Spanish trip had taken most of the money. The thought of how she'd raised it so Deborah could have the 'sun, sea and sand' the brochure had promised strengthened her resolve. Kathryn was very aware of the restive movements among the other tourists waiting behind her.

"The manager is busy," the receptionist was saying. "He cannot see anyone."

Kathryn leaned forward. "I'm staying here until he does see me," she informed him with quiet ice.

Some of his urbanity slipped. "You

are making much over little, Señora."
His voice rose. "All these people being
delayed! You are not fair!"

"Fair!" Kathryn's anger spilled over.
"What would you know . . . "

"What's going on here?" A new
voice demanded from behind Kathryn.
"What's the problem?"

She and the courier swung round.
Two men were heading across the
crowded foyer. The questioner, of
medium height, thin, his bony face
deeply tanned, repeated his demand
on reaching the counter, his probing
gaze switching from Kathryn to the
receptionist then back. His companion
halted a pace to the side.

"Are you the manager?" Kathryn
asked, preparing to tackle the newcomer.

The black-haired man hesitated,
glanced towards the older one at
his shoulder, and said, "I'm Rafael
Delvega. What is the problem?"

"Over booking!" Kathryn was beyond
caution or good manners. "It's scan-
dalous to treat people like this."

4

"Ah, yes!" Rafael Delvega threw the older man a look which would have quailled a tiger. A snapped order produced a typed list which he read before addressing the patient queue of holiday-makers. "Due to an unfortunate administrative error certain rooms were double booked. To make amends I have reserved accommodation at another hotel. It is larger and has more amenities than this one."

The listed guests raised several questions before accepting the change. Kathryn noticed no children were named except Deborah. She looked at her seven-year-old daughter, the pallor of ill health showing beneath the tiredness. Blonde hair, darker than her mother's, drooped limply on her forehead. "Can't we stay here?" she whispered.

A sense of failure oppressed Kathryn. She had wanted this first holiday to be perfect not the mess it was turning into.

"Shall we get on the coach now?"

Someone asked from the back.

"If you please." A shrivelling look directed at the older man sent him scurrying to shepherd the small group out of the foyer and on to the waiting vehicle.

"Señora?" Rafael Delvega was once more at her side. "All is resolved?"

"No doubt for you!" Full of angry frustration, Kathryn picked up her bag. "You have slid out of it all quite neatly, Señor Delvega. It isn't you who will have to explain to a young child why she is so far from the sea."

"There is a swimming-pool," he began.

"Which is not the same as the sea and a beach!" Kathryn found their suitcase. "There is no point in protesting any longer. You've no interest or consideration, ruining our holiday without even an apology. It is a disgraceful way to run a business. In your place I would be thoroughly ashamed." Kathryn struggled to lift the heavy case. "Come on, Deb, or

6

the coach will go without us."

"Wait!" Rafael Delvega's face had tightened with a deep sprung anger. "I can assure you, Señora, I did everything to rectify the mistake once it was brought to my notice."

"As the manager you should have a better grip on things," Kathryn bitterly accused. "Why didn't you give some notification of the change instead of letting us find out this way. It would have given people time to cancel. I certainly would!" She dropped the case in order to change hands. "Or maybe you didn't want to risk that happening so you took the money and said nothing."

Kathryn knew she had gone too far but the circumstances made her unrepentant. She faced the glowering Spaniard in an unyielding mood. Staring into his set features, Kathryn had the oddest sensation his anger was nothing to do with her at all. It was turned on himself.

The lift doors closed behind the

last of the guests and the receptionist disappeared into the room behind the counter. The oppressive hush was broken by the return of the older man. He asked a hesitant question and was rewarded by a harsh negative. He hastily backed out and Rafael Delvega took the case from Kathryn.

"Come with me," he requested, turned on his heel and strode across, the foyer in the direction of the office. Outside an engine started then the coach drove past the open doors. Kathryn rushed after the retreating man. "The coach has gone without us!"

"I know." He dropped the case beside a padded bench. "Sit down for a moment."

"Why? What are you doing?" The words came out in great agitation. "What's going on?"

"Señora Morris, for once, don't argue." He was now more aloof than angry. "Please sit down."

Unexpectedly the strain of the day

8

wilted Kathryn and she slumped on to the bench. He went into the office and all was quiet again.

"Mum?" Deborah huddled against Kathryn, the tears threatening. "Have we got to go home?"

Kathryn put an arm round the weary child and pushed back the damp hair. "No," she denied, "Señor Delvega will sort it out for us."

He'd better, she thought, although not relishing another passage of arms with the forceful Spaniard. Deborah settled drowsily in her hold whilst Kathryn was equally glad of the chance of a rest. They had left home early for a tiresome journey to reach the airport only to find their flight was delayed for two hours. Because of it their arrival coincided with the greatest heat of the day. Worn out by excitement and lack of sleep Deborah had grown more and more tense. She'd clutched her mother's hand too overwhelmed to speak. Kathryn was assailed by the agonising doubt that the Spanish holiday was a huge mistake. Better to have stayed in England than have a miserable time here in Spain.

Leaning back, eyes closed, Kathryn experienced a rare bout of deep loneliness. Being a one-parent family was far from easy, the responsibility weighing very heavy at times. Lost in thought, she missed the opening of the office door.

"Señora Morris." Kathryn jerked out of her abstraction to find Rafael Delvega regarding her with a detached expression. "All is arranged." He picked up the case. "If you are ready I'll take you."

Without moving Kathryn said: "Where to?"

"A place a little further up the coast by the sea with a good beach." He held out his free hand. "Come, Señora. The arrangements are made and your daughter looks too tired to be out of bed any longer."

The truth robbed Kathryn of the desire to argue any more. Taking

Deborah's hand, she followed him to the rear access where he swung the case into the boot of an elderly blue Seat. The man checked their doors were locked then eased behind the driving wheel. This close Kathryn could see he was a little younger than she'd first supposed, maybe thirtyish, with cropped black hair ruffled back from well-defined features.

He looked across to catch her staring. A faint smile appeared which lightened the severe expression. "Don't worry, Señora. This time I have it right."

He started the car and drove along the side of the hotel. Kathryn could see the Christoval had a rather run-down appearance, being badly in need of a coat of paint and some general repairs.

Hugging the shore the road climbed out of the town. Across the molten blue, the sea hazed into the July sky. Over it all lay the shimmering cloak of afternoon heat. Perspiration prickled on Kathryn's shoulders and she longed for a bath. "How long before we arrive?" she asked the silent man at her side.

"Not too far." The road turned inland away from the side-by-side march of tourist hotels.

Several miles later the car slowed to take a turn off. A large board advertised the Hotel Mediterraneo further along the side road. Kathryn gazed eagerly ahead anxious to catch a first glimpse of the place.

It was large and very expensive-looking with shrubs and benches dotted about the extensive grounds. Spread on the clifftop, the hotel was clearly a luxurious establishment. Kathryn's mouth dried in shock. She thought of their one suitcase and its contents, totally inadequate for such surroundings.

Near to the entrance from the road Kathryn gathered her wits. "Señor Delvega," she began.

"*Si.*" He flipped a quick look in her direction — and drove past the hotel entrance and up an incline.

Taken aback Kathryn stuttered, "Er . . . nothing."

At the far aside of the incline Rafael Delvega turned into a dusty driveway which led to a white house set into the slope facing the sea. "We are here," he announced and got out.

Startled Kathryn gazed at what could only be a private house. The car doors were opened for her and Deborah. She followed him to the boot. "I don't understand! Whose house is this?"

With his back to her, bending over, his reply was muffled. She thought he said it belonged to the hotel although she wasn't sure. Intent on questioning him further, she was frustrated by a woman coming from the house. She reached the car with a joking remark in Spanish. The warmth in the man's answering smile altered his whole expression. The newcomer was short, comfortably built, middle sixties with grey-streaked hair and wonderfully impish eyes.

"This is Anna," Rafael Delvega

introduced. "She doesn't speak English but I expect you'll manage. Anna looks after the house and cooks like a dream."

The two women shook hands, sizing one another up. Anna's gaze dropped to Deborah and her smile disappeared. An order was sent in the man's direction and he hastily collected the case from the car. Anna hustled Kathryn and Deborah into the house, muttering most of the time. A door was flung back to reveal a tiled bathroom before she led them to a bedroom where the blinds were closed against the sun.

Bringing the suitcase, Rafael Delvega walked into a stream of words. "Anna says she will fetch you a cool drink while you see to the child. Leave the unpacking until you have rested."

Kathryn drifted back to wakefulness with a pleasurable slowness. Stretching out a hand she checked her watch on the bedside table. She'd slept for three hours. Yawning a little she crossed the polished floor to the window and peered round the blind. The sun was well *en route* for the horizon, edges blurred, force spent. It was a beautiful evening, too good to waste in bed. Kathryn unpacked then dressed in a cotton skirt and sleeveless top.

She sighed over her paleness. No use to bother over it, she'd never tanned and never would. Kathryn had got used to her fair looks, the light blonde hair, the brows and lashes that had to be darkened to show up and the skin that rarely varied in tone.

"I'm like a blank canvas waiting to be painted on," she had long ago moaned to her husband.

"Not with those eyes!" Colin had chuckled. They were her best feature, brilliant blue, twinkly when she was happy, luminous when sad. They lit her face, lifting it from the plain to one people remembered.

Deborah slept on soundly and Kathryn decided to leave her. The house was very quiet and a quick search showed it was empty. The house was small, furnished in a homely way. The room she was sharing with Deborah and the living-room overlooked the sea.

The kitchen, bathroom and the main bedroom formed the back of the house. Kathryn retreated quickly from the latter room feeling she'd trespassed. It bore signs of use and she didn't want to annoy anyone.

"The sound of a car brought her away from enjoying the seascape afforded by the living-room windows. Rafael Delvega was at the door by the time she opened it. He'd changed tailored slacks and tie for a tee-shirt and denims, looking more tourist than resident.

"Hello again," he greeted, surveying her critically. He ambled across the room and pushed open the door leading on to a terrace that ran the length of the house. "Have you had a good look round?"

"I've just got up," Kathryn replied diplomatically.

"The house is simple enough." He dismissed it with a wave. "Come

16

outside." The roof extended over the terrace to give it shade. A table and some chairs occupied part of it. "I recommend breakfast out here. It's a great way to start the day."

A small wrought-iron gate broke the line of the terrace wall giving access to a flight of wooden steps that dog-legged to the beach. Half-way down Rafael Delvega stopped so Kathryn could see everything. Two outcrops of rock formed a tiny bay. The house was set on the hillside between them having the little beach to itself. From where they stood a path went off to one of the headlands. The steps continued down to the beach.

Kathryn was enchanted with the quiet beauty of the secluded bay. "It is all right our being here, isn't it?" She was afraid it would be snatched away.

"Didn't I tell you everything was arranged." He smiled at her. "Where is Deborah?"

"Still asleep. The journey overtired her." She walked by his side along the beach. "The doctor said she needed a holiday with plenty of sun and fresh air."

"Now I understand the onslaught at the hotel!" They'd reached the end of the beach, it was only forty yards or so. "It really had to be the seaside."

"Yes, it really did." Before starting to walk back Kathryn said, "I spoke in anger this afternoon for which I apologise. I want the best for Deborah, she's been so ill but there was no need . . ."

"Don't worry about it," he interrupted. "You were right to complain."

They slowly retraced their steps. "I wondered if I'd been too ambitious in coming to Spain. We could only just afford it."

"Is that why your husband is not with you?"

Kathryn paused, one foot on the bottom step. "He died a while ago. There's only Deborah and me."

Instead of the conventional 'I'm sorry," Rafael Delvega said, "And life

18

has been hard since then." It was a statement not a question.

Kathryn mounted the step so their faces were on a level. "Certainly not easy," she conceded, "but I have Deborah and she's worth the struggle."

The hillside around the house was dotted with shrubs and small trees. To the right a belt of mature trees obscured the house from the luxury hotel on the other side of the incline.

Kathryn could see the top storey from where she stood. Faint music was drifting on the evening breeze. "Is it always this quiet?" she asked.

"Usually." Smoothing a patch of sand, he started to draw on it. "This back road turns off and comes past the Mediterraneo then the house continuing through the village and rejoining the coast road further on. The village is just over a kilometre from here."

He straightened up. "Anna lives there and comes every day. If you walk to the main road you can get a bus to town." With a last glance towards the sun-dappled sea, he said, "Let's see what Anna has left for you to eat?"

Anna had left enough for a feast, let alone two small appetites. "We'll never get through all this," Kathryn protested, looking at the array of dishes. On impulse, she asked, "Have you eaten?"

The man shook his head. "Haven't had time yet?"

"Would you like some?" A belated thought struck her. "That is if you're not expected at home."

"I'll join you. We'll have it outside."

Kathryn checked on her sleeping daughter while he carried plates and dishes to the terrace. Deborah hadn't stirred and Kathryn sat on the side of the bed. So precious a child, reminder of her parents' brief youthful marriage.

"Deborah still asleep?" Rafael Delvega inquired on Kathryn's return to the kitchen.

"Like a hibernating mouse," she replied.

On the terrace he pulled out a chair for Kathryn. "She will be fine tomorrow. You need have no worries for the beach is clean and there are no currents off the rocks further out. Can she swim yet?"

Kathryn sat down. "Very well. I'm an instructor so she learned young."

The food was delicious. Kathryn felt all her anxieties slipping away, a relaxed well-being filling her mind. "Are you a local, Señor Delvega?" she asked towards the end of the meal.

"Yes," he answered, pushing aside his empty plate.

"Your English is excellent. Where did you learn?"

"My father's sister married an Englishman. I used to stay with them frequently as a child." He poured more fruit juice. "Where do you live?"

"In the Midlands near Coventry." Kathryn looked out to sea where the setting sun was laying molten red across the water's surface. "It's totally different to this."

Following her gaze he warned, "Don't let the spectacle blind you to the danger. Come off the beach at midday and stay out of the sun for the afternoon. It must be treated with respect at its zenith."

"At all times by me," Kathryn confessed ruefully. "Fortunately Deborah tans beautifully."

He frowned. "You must be careful. Heatstroke is most unpleasant."

"I'm fully prepared," Kathryn assured him. "I don't intend to spoil my holiday."

Later Rafael Delvega said good-bye and left. "Get a decent night's sleep," was his parting remark.

Kathryn spent an hour on the terrace watching the sea deepen to a velvety darkness before going to bed. Lying on top of the sheet she congratulated herself on how well everything had turned out.

★ ★ ★

She woke early the next morning. Dressing in linen trousers and a loose long-sleeved top, Kathryn left the bedroom and located her daughter in the kitchen with Anna.

"*Buenos dias*," she greeted Kathryn with a beaming smile.

Kathryn tried a tentative, "*Buenos dias*," and the smile broadened.

"Mum! Look what Anna has brought me to play with." Deborah held up a large wooden train whose chipped paintwork testified to plentiful usage.

"*Gracias*, Anna." Kathryn wished she could say more.

"Can I use it on the beach?" Deborah asked.

Kathryn mimed taking the train down on to the sand and Anna nodded vigorously.

"We'll go now." Deborah took her mother's hand, anxious to see the delights of this new place.

"Sun cream first," Kathryn insisted. "Even the early morning sun is strong."

Deborah spread a generous layer on

her arms and legs while Kathryn fetched their hats, her own a wide-brimmed affair that threw a deep shadow over her face.

"Where does that go?" Deborah stopped where the steps turned.

"Let's see." Kathryn followed her daughter.

The path led on to the headland. A rocky shelf jutted out over the water and had a diving-board bolted on to it.

"Can we try it later?" Deborah begged.

"When I've checked the depth." Kathryn was firm. "You could end up with a flat head."

Deborah laughed and hitched the train under one arm. She was delighted with the beach, kicking off her sandals and paddling in the water. Kathryn made sure they climbed the steps slowly. Even so Deborah was out of breath, the colour ebbing from her face. Kathryn stifled her worry. Time, the doctor had said.

Anna left soon after breakfast having shown Kathryn food for the rest of the day.

"What's in that?" Deborah asked, sniffing at a savoury flan.

"I'm not sure." Kathryn put it into the large fridge. "We'll have to try it to see."

They changed into swimsuits and returned to the beach. Kathryn watched the time not wanting to overdo the first session. "We can come again later."

"I'm not a bit tired," Deborah declared. "Shall we walk up the road a bit."

Kathryn turned back when she felt they'd gone a reasonable distance. The countryside was brown and rather uninteresting with little to see.

"I'm tired now," Deborah admitted as they went up the drive to the house. "The sun's really hot."

"We'll have lunch then a siesta," Kathryn said.

"See who?"

Kathryn laughed and explained.

"Seems funny to go to bed in the afternoon."

"You don't have to," Kathryn smiled. "Read quietly for a bit."

Deborah lay on the bed to read a comic and was soon asleep. Kathryn changed into a sleeveless dress and took a book to the living-room. A heavy silence pervaded the atmosphere as if the very land slept beneath the baking rays of a merciless sun. Kathryn let her thoughts drift in lazy circles. Rafael Delvega was a kindly man, she decided. She felt sorely in need of a little kindness. This time last year was when the letter had arrived.

At first she had not believed what was written there. Compulsory purchase! Finding the neighbours on either side were similarly affected brought little comfort. Their house was rented. Where would they live after the landlord was forced to sell?

The council housing officer was a brisk man with a professional smile. "Of course we'll re-house you, Mrs

26

Morris. I'll be in touch."

Weeks of worry ended with the allocation of a flat on the edge of a small estate. Moving house in the bleak February had been a strain yet worse was to come. She'd thought Deborah's listlessness was due to missing her friends and starting a new school. When that explanation could not possibly be true, Kathryn consulted a doctor. A series of tests were made as Deborah lost weight at a frightening rate.

The night the ambulance had come was the worst of Kathryn's life. The way to recovery was so slow she often despaired. When the doctor had discharged Deborah he'd spoken of a holiday.

"Can we go to Spain?" Deborah had asked. "Lots of people at school have been."

So Kathryn rashly promised Spain knowing full well she shouldn't have done. Now it looked as though their world had righted itself. The flat was fairly new with central heating and a fitted kitchen. It was nearer to her work so she saved on fares. Yes, thought Kathryn in drowsy contentment, everything is well again.

★ ★ ★

The squeal of tyres and slamming of car doors jerked Kathryn from her seat. She hurried to look through the kitchen window. Half a dozen teenagers were gathered round a coupé talking noisily. Annoyed at the shattering of the afternoon calm, Kathryn went out of the back door to see who they were. The youngsters were surprised by her appearance. One of the boys threw a remark at a dark-haired girl wearing a shirt over a bikini. The girl rapped out a question in Spanish at Kathryn.

"I don't understand," she said. "I'm English."

"Who are you?" the girl asked with a heavy accent.

"I'm staying here," Kathryn replied. "Who are you?"

"I am Teresa." The girl frowned. "Why you here?"

"From the hotel." Kathryn tried to keep it simple for the girl to follow. "The hotel was full."

"Hotel!" Teresa latched on to a word she recognised.

Kathryn smiled. "Yes, from the hotel."

"My cousin own hotel," the girl flatly declared. "She not know you here."

Kathryn's smile vanished. "But the manager said everything was arranged!"

Her words went straight past the Spanish girl, face set with temper. "My cousin not like you here. I tell her." She stalked to the car. "My cousin tell you go."

"Wait!" Kathryn hurried forward.

The car hurtled away in a churning of dust leaving Kathryn in a daze. It was one thing to stand firm over a hotel booking but in a private house? What could she do? Where would they go?

The sudden shrilling of the phone in the kitchen made her jump. Kathryn hesitated over answering it. Finally she picked it up.

"Rafael Delvega here." He seemed very close. "I called to see how you are doing. Are you both well?"

"No, we are not!" Kathryn cried in anguish. "How could you do this? Making us believe we could spend our holiday here! How could you be . . . " The emotion nearly engulfed her.

"What do you mean? What has happened?" The questions came fast. "Are you still there? Answer me!"

"Teresa came a while ago and told me the truth. We will have to leave." A movement outside caught her eye. A sleek green car turned off the road and pulled up by the house.

"Listen to me, Señora Morris." The voice in her ear became more urgent.

"No!" Kathryn saw a fashionably dressed woman emerge from the driving seat. "I listened to you yesterday and look what's happened. The hotel owner

30

is here now. I hope you're satisfied."

Kathryn slammed down the phone and took a deep breath. She felt sick at the thought of telling her daughter they'd got to move out.

Footsteps sounded then a sharp rap on the door. With dragging feet Kathryn went to open it.

2

"*BUENAS tardas.*" The woman walked past the apprehensive Kathryn. "I am Olivia Santini. My cousin told me of your presence. What are you doing in this house?" Her English was good with an attractive accent.

Shutting the door Kathryn said, "My name is Morris. My daughter and I are on holiday from England. At the Christoval there was a double booking. I complained to the manager and he said we could stay here."

"The manager?" Olivia Santini queried.

"Yes," Kathryn quickly confirmed. "Rafael Delvega."

An eyebrow was lifted. "Miguel Perrera is the manager of the Christoval."

Kathryn caught her breath. "Señor Delvega said . . . " She stopped and frowned in concentration. Had he definitely said he was the Christoval's manager?

"Let us sit down and discuss this properly," Olivia Santini suggested. "It all sounds very confusing."

Kathryn followed her into the living-room, perching uneasily on the edge of her seat as the other woman reclined gracefully in a high-backed chair. Making sure all was included, Kathryn recounted the events of the previous afternoon.

Olivia Santini digested the account and eventually smiled briefly. "All is explained. We have had trouble in the past with tourists from your country who arrive without booked accommodation. They often sleep on the beaches but there have been instances where vacant houses have been taken over."

"Squatters!" Kathryn was not pleased.

"Teresa was most insistent someone was here unauthorised. I came as soon as possible ready to call the police should it be necessary."

"And now?" Kathryn asked anxiously.

The woman waved a dismissive hand. "My young cousin is inclined to be dramatic and make much of little."

Kathryn couldn't relax. "About our staying here . . ."

The hand was waved again. "Rafael is generous to a fault. I am sure he will tell me about it at dinner this evening. I have just returned from Madrid and have not seen him for a week."

"I wouldn't want to be the cause of any bother," Kathryn said. She had the feeling this well-groomed woman would have a formidable temper.

"My dear Señora Morris," Olivia Santini was all graciousness. "Rafael and I have been very close for years. I would not dream of interfering."

She crossed her legs and smiled with such assurance Kathryn felt like an awkward teenager. The Spanish woman was more striking than beautiful, the carefully casual hairstyle softening her hard jawline and making the most of a wide forehead and dark eyes. Her cotton dress was a world apart from the simple one Kathryn was wearing. Several gold chains and a pair of ornate earrings added the finishing touch. Kathryn judged the woman to be two or three years older than herself, perhaps thirty, though it was difficult to be sure.

Olivia Santini rose and went to the open door on to the terrace. "I love the sea. It is always a relief to get back from the city." She glanced over her shoulder. "How long will your stay be?"

"Two weeks," Kathryn replied. "At least Señor Delvega said we could but if he's not the manager of . . ."

"He is my manager," the other woman interrupted. "I own the Hotel Mediterraneo."

Kathryn's eyes widened in surprise. Up to now she'd thought the woman was connected to the Christoval.

"I have my own suite and live there for most of the year, though Rafael

35

runs everything so smoothly it would not matter if I never saw the place at all."

The bedroom door opened and Deborah peeped round. Kathryn beckoned her in. "This is my daughter."

Olivia Santini looked her over. "What a little wisp she is!" A hand went to her mouth. "Oh, dear! I should not have said that. It is just that my Luis is so sturdy others appear undersized."

"Deborah hasn't been well," Kathryn reminded the other woman.

With quiet complacency Olivia Santini said, "Luis is rarely ill." Her expression contained more than a hint of superiority. "An ailing child is such a liability, do you not find?"

Kathryn felt a whispering of dislike for the elegant Spaniard and sought to suppress the dawning emotion. "I expect you're right," she answered neutrally.

With a glance at her watch the other woman said she must leave. "I have to change for dinner. It does not do to keep a man waiting too long."

Kathryn watched the green car drive away with some misgivings. She didn't like being beholden to Olivia Santini whose general attitude had not been to her taste. Then there was the business of Rafael Delvega. His being at the Christoval had not been explained nor the offering of the house. He must indeed be very close to Olivia Santini if he could behave with such confidence where she was concerned. Kathryn found it all very perplexing.

* * *

Half an hour later the old Seat came to an abrupt halt in the drive. Through the kitchen window Kathryn saw Rafael Delvega striding towards the house and put down the plates she was holding.

"Shall we get this straightened out," he said the moment he was inside.

"There was no need for you to rush over," Kathryn informed him. "Everything is straightened out. Señora

Santini was very kind and said the arrangement could stand."

An expression of amusement came to his face. "That *was* kind of her!"

Kathryn found his reaction puzzling. "What's the matter?" she demanded.

The question was ignored. "Tell me about Teresa's visit?" He listened intently. "Knowing Teresa she hot-footed to her cousin anxious to divert attention from herself. She's not supposed to bring people here."

"I hope she won't get into trouble," Kathryn said. "No harm was done and everything is out in the open."

"Out in the open! You make it sound under-handed!"

"You know what I mean." Kathryn was irritated. "The house belongs to the hotel and it's scarcely fair staying here without Señora Santini's knowledge."

Very quietly Rafael Delvega said, "The Mediterraneo is Olivia's concern, this house is not. Who stays here is none of her business."

Mind whirling Kathryn thought back

38

to their arrival. "You mean the house belongs to the Christoval?"

"No." The denial was firm. "It belongs to me."

"You!" Kathryn was taken aback. "Why didn't you make that clear yesterday?"

"Because you wouldn't have accepted the offer!" He saw from her expression he was right. "I took one look at your daughter and knew I couldn't send you to the other hotel as I had planned." He spread his hands in a gesture of appeal. "Now tell me I did the wrong thing!"

Kathryn was won over immediately. "It was a very generous action and I thank you most sincerely, Señor Delvega. But where are you staying?"

"No problem." He leaned a shoulder against a tall cupboard. "I live-in with my job."

"At the Mediterraneo? Señora Santini said you were the manager there."

He nodded, a certain wariness in his face. "What else did she say?"

"Not much." Kathryn took some

food Anna had left from the fridge. "She seemed confused by my thinking you were the manager of the Christoval."

She waited for an explanation but none came. Instead he asked, "Have you everything you need?"

"Certainly. The house is very comfortable and Anna prepares enough food for six."

"She told me you both need feeding up." He looked around. "Where's your daughter?"

She was on the terrace colouring a picture with a selection of felt-tip pens. Rafael Delvega sat beside her and commented on her efforts. Deborah was pleased by his praise and smiled shyly at him.

"Can I call you Deborah?" he inquired.

She managed a quiet "Yes," quite overcome by his indulgent interest.

"You can call me Rafael." He glanced over to Kathryn. "So can you, Señora Morris."

"Mum's name is Kathryn," Deborah

revealed in a rush of confidence and was delighted when he leant over and said, "It's a good Spanish name."

He stood up. "I've got a business meeting in half an hour so I'd better go." He pulled a paper from his pocket and handed it to Kathryn. "That's my office number at the Mediterraneo. Give me a ring if you have a problem."

They went to see him off. At the car he said, "Teresa comes here sometimes with Olivia's son, Luis. She's employed to look after him. The hotel frontage is all rocks and Luis likes the beach."

"Isn't he nice, Mum," Deborah said waving goodbye.

"Yes," Kathryn agreed, wondering if Olivia Santini knew she was regarded as business by her manager. She had hinted the relationship was a lot warmer than that.

* * *

"Are we going to try the diving-board?" Deborah asked at breakfast the following morning.

"We can check the pool," Kathryn answered. "There's plenty of time. It's only seven o'clock."

"Seems later." Deborah finished a glass of fruit juice. "We don't breakfast this early at home."

"We don't go to bed in the afternoon, either," Kathryn grinned.

Chuckling they went to the beach. The water was pale beneath the strengthening sun, the air lacking the stifling heat the coming hours would bring. A breeze flitted across the water surface causing small waveless to lap around the rocks at the end of the sand.

"I am glad Rafael let us stay here." Deborah removed her sandals. "A whole beach to ourselves."

"We're very lucky." Kathryn smoothed back her daughter's hair. "By the time we go home you'll be as brown as a nutmeg and bursting with health."

"Take lots of photos," Deborah reminded her, "so I can take them to school. I bet nobody else has their own beach." She paddled at the water's edge.

Kathryn waded in. "Let's go round to the rock pool and see what it's like."

With Deborah in front they swam to the other side of the jutting pile of rocks and into the pool over which the diving-board was bolted. "Be careful near the rocks," Kathryn warned. "They have sharp edges. I'm going to look below."

The water was fairly clear and a lot deeper than she'd expected. It took a while to check the whole pool but Kathryn persevered. Surfacing for the last time she held up both thumbs. "All clear."

"Let's give it a try." The youngster was off without waiting for a reply.

Kathryn soon overhauled her. "No need to rush."

They both sat on the sand to rest before tackling the short climb up the path. Once on the diving-board

Deborah's nerve temporarily deserted her. "You go first," she told her mother.

Kathryn contented herself with a straightforward dive off the board. There was still ample water beneath her when she struck for the surface.

"I'm coming," Deborah shouted. She created a considerable splash and came up giggling.

After a couple more times Kathryn called a halt. She didn't want her daughter getting too tired.

In the late afternoon they returned to the diving-board, Deborah jumping off with youthful zest to see how big a splash she could make. Kathryn was much more sedate.

"Do some somersaults," Deborah urged, sitting on a rock by the board to rest.

The first dive was a mess with a lot of over-rotation. Concentrating hard she tried again, executing the single twist with something like her old precision. She surfaced feeling pleased with herself. Swimming round to the beach she found Deborah waiting with Rafael.

"I didn't know you were a champion diver," he greeted.

Kathryn slicked back her hair. "I used to do a lot at one time but I'm out of practice now." She picked up a towel. "Have you come to collect something from the house?"

"No. To bring you a useful item." He turned. "Come and see."

He was only wearing shorts and sandals, the deep allover tan contrasting with their pale skins. His body and thighs carried a reasonable layer of muscle although, to Kathryn's critical eye, he seemed a bit underweight. Tired too, she thought, studying his face as he opened the boot of the car. Had the 'business' meeting finished late?

"What is it?" Deborah watched intrigued as Rafael took a large holdall from the boot.

"You'll see!" The lid was slammed shut. "Go into the kitchen and fetch the key hanging by the door."

The key opened a small store room built on to the back of the house. Rafael brought out two padded loungers and a collapsible table. "More comfortable than sitting on the sand," he told Kathryn. "You take these and I'll bring the bag."

"It's a tent!" Deborah squealed when the contents of the holdall were revealed.

"A sort of beach shelter." Rafael spread out the metal poles. They assembled into a frame some six feet high and about twelve long. A cover clipped on to the top to create a fair-sized shadow on the sand. "Saves keep going up to the house when you've had enough of the sun. It belongs to a friend who won't be needing it for a couple of months."

Deborah was enchanted. "It is like a tent."

Kathryn sat on a lounger and smiled up at Rafael. "Utter luxury! You're spoiling us."

"Not really! The stuff is available so why not use it." He beckoned to Deborah. "I've brought someone for you to play with."

She was surprised. "I didn't see anyone."

"Hiding from you!"

"Why?" Deborah was brimming with anticipation.

"Very shy." Rafael walked towards the steps.

Deborah went after him. "Who is it?"

The reply was lost to Kathryn. She swung her legs on to a lounger and stared across the sea. The water made a soft sucking noise where it met the sand, a gentle murmuring that was very restful.

"Mum!" Deborah's excited shout brought Kathryn upright. "Look what Rafael's given me!"

The inflatable duck was large and bright red, its eyes outrageously long-lashed and with a cheeky up-tilt to the yellow beak.

"From another friend?" Kathryn smiled at Rafael.

"His children have outgrown it," he assured her.

"I shall call it Daffy like the one on T.V." Deborah could hardly get her arms round the big inflatable. "I'm taking it in the sea." She was off in a rush.

Kathryn was on her feet. "Come back at once."

The unusually stern voice halted the running child. She turned, saw her mother's expression and came back with equal speed. Placing a hand on her daughter's shoulder Kathryn held Deborah's gaze. "You are *never* to take the duck into the sea unless I'm here. It's very easy to drift away on something like that and I don't want you floating out to sea."

"I promise!" Deborah said in so earnest a tone her mother's mouth twitched.

Kathryn let her go. "Now you can go into the sea."

Rafael came to stand beside Kathryn. "I was going to warn Deborah myself if you hadn't."

"I shall keep a close watch." They saw the duck roll over pitching Deborah into the water with a loud shriek. "Thank you for both the duck and the shelter."

He ran a hand round the back of his neck, flexing his shoulders. "I want you to enjoy your stay."

"I'm sure we will." Kathryn squinted at the sun. "I'll have to get in the shade. Sit down if you're not in a hurry to be off." He really did look tired.

"Thank you." Rafael sprawled on the other lounger, sandals left on the sand. "I could do with some peace. It's been a rather hectic twenty-four hours."

"Do you get much time off?" Kathryn asked.

"Now is the busy season so we work slightly longer hours." Settling more comfortably he continued, "The hotel employs temporary staff at this time and they need closer supervision than the regular ones."

"You seem young to be the manager of a hotel that size," Kathryn commented. "How long has it been?"

"Three years," he replied. "I was the deputy manager and took over when Olivia's father died. He'd sold two smaller hotels to finance the Mediterraneo which opened about seven years ago."

"Mum! Come and play." Deborah was waving energetically. "It's great fun." She laughed uproariously when the duck sank under her mother's weight.

"Watch me." Deborah scrambled on to the duck's back and paddled with her feet.

A stout cord was tied to the duck's neck which was useful for towing. Kathryn wore herself out pulling her daughter through the shallows. "We'll bring the duck down again tomorrow."

"Look," the little girl whispered. "Rafael's asleep."

"We won't wake him," Kathryn

whispered back. "Go up to the house and get our books."

Deborah left on the errand and Kathryn put the duck under the shelter out of the sun. Rafael slept on, his head turned to one side, body totally relaxed. Kathryn remembered how vulnerable her husband had always looked when asleep. Not this man! The facial bones were too pronounced giving him an appearance of strength despite the lack of expression on his tanned features. Even like this he had the mien of a man who knew exactly what he was doing and where he was going.

★ ★ ★

An hour afterwards Kathryn gently shook him into wakefulness. "I didn't know how long to leave you."

Rafael was alert at once, raking back his hair and checking the time. "Didn't mean to flake out on you."

"We're going up to eat now and you won't want to be left here." She folded the loungers and Rafael carried them to the store room.

"The shelter will be all right on the beach," he told Kathryn. "Take the cover off if the wind gets up otherwise the frame could be damaged."

Kathryn sat on the terrace with a pot of coffee watching the day turn into night. A soft darkness hid the harsh contours of the rocks and seemed just made for strolling hand-in-hand along the deserted beach.

Smiling at her fanciful imaginings, she poured more coffee and tried to dismiss the scene. Kathryn had been out with several men since her husband's death but nothing serious. Most faded when they learned of Deborah, not wanting to be bothered with another man's child. None had upset Kathryn for her heart had not been involved but she did wonder if she was destined to spend the rest of her life without a partner.

Kathryn gave herself a mental shake. Such depressing thoughts were not for so lovely a night. She sent them packing and turned her mind to the next day. She'd like to visit the nearby town where the Christoval was. On that positive note Kathryn went to bed.

* * *

Deborah was quite happy to go to town for the morning but, in the end, they didn't. Teresa arrived during breakfast with a small boy in tow. She pointed at him and said, "He Luis."

Olivia's six-year-old was tall for his age and quite sturdy though a less charitable observer would have said plump. His dark hair fell in a thick fringe on to his round face and well to his shoulders at the back. He did indeed make Deborah look a wisp of a child. They eyed each other with a cautious interest.

"We swim," Teresa said to Kathryn.

Behind the girl Kathryn saw the disapproving look on Anna's face. A few minutes later the living-room rugs were taken outside to be soundly beaten, Anna's annoyance finding release in furious action.

At first Kathryn took no notice of the screaming for children's play can be extremely noisy. Then, in a gap in the conversation with Deborah, the pitch triggered a mental alarm and she jerked round. A loud scream came again. Fear, not enjoyment! Kathryn was on her feet immediately, running for the steps. It was coming from the right where the diving-board was. She rushed on to the ledge overlooking the pool.

Luis was on the end of the board, his tear-streaked face crumpled with fright. In the middle of the board, blocking his passage to safety, was Teresa. Intent on her taunting she missed Kathryn's arrival.

"Leave him," Kathryn ordered. "Get off the board."

Teresa glanced round and pouted but didn't move from her position.

With great emphasis Kathryn repeated, "Get off."

54

The girl may not have understood the words, the meaning she knew at once. She glared at Kathryn then came nonchalantly off the board and leant against a rock.

Kathryn stood on the board and held out a hand. "Come on, Luis."

The boy was sniffing and gulping. Kathryn went forward, picked him up and carried him to the ledge.

"Is he all right, Mum?" Deborah asked anxiously.

Kathryn put the boy down. "Just a bit frightened."

"Him big baby," Teresa said in contempt.

Kathryn swung round jabbing a finger in the girl's direction. "You are also a big baby," she snapped.

Teresa flushed and let loose something in her own language before stalking up the path.

"What did she say?" Deborah was bewildered.

"Probably telling me to mind my own business!"

The three of them went along the path to its junction with the steps. They could see Teresa on the beach stripping off her shorts and shirt before wading into the water and striking out strongly. She took her child-minding duties rather lightly, Kathryn thought in exasperation. One look at Luis' face showed she couldn't leave him on the beach to wait for Teresa's return.

"We'll stay here this morning," she told Deborah.

"O.K!" Deborah wasn't concerned. "Let's get the stuff for the beach."

Luis sniffed all the way to the house but brightened when he saw the train Anna had given Deborah. He carried it to the beach and was inclined to monopolise it. Deborah didn't take kindly to this and, in spite of the language barrier, made him understand he had to share. Harmony restored, the two played together.

Teresa came back shaking the water from herself and wringing the long hair.

She went over to Luis and spoke to him. Eventually he nodded and she patted his shoulder.

"We friends," Teresa said joining Kathryn under the shelter. "Luis he difficult. Make trouble." She knelt on the sand. "Olivia very busy."

Kathryn put down her book. "How old are you?"

Teresa drew the number seventeen in the sand. She moved over to sunbathe and Kathryn returned to her book. Deborah came to fetch the inflatable duck which had lain under the shelter all night. Luis wanted it for himself. Although a year younger Luis was as tall as the girl and heavier. Deborah abandoned confrontation for guile and took the duck into the sea. Luis promptly threw a tantrum at the water's edge.

Kathryn was amazed at the violence of his reaction. Screaming at Teresa he jumped up and down in his rage. Deborah gazed open-mouthed at the storm she'd raised. Teresa went over but failed to calm him. She waved to Deborah to bring the duck on to the sand. The girl shook her head and Luis renewed his howls.

In irritation Teresa grabbed one arm and all but dragged him across the beach to the steps. His crying faded into the distance leaving Kathryn feeling she may have misjudged Teresa. The job was no sinecure.

"I'm hungry." Deborah put down the wet duck. "Can we eat?"

Kathryn was surprised by Anna still being at the house. She usually left mid-morning. By gestures Anna indicated she'd stayed because Teresa and Luis had come. She pointed to the phone and dialled.

"This is Rafael." The now familiar voice came in Kathryn's ear. "I rang earlier when you were on the beach. What have you planned for Thursday? Would you like to look round Almeria? I have to go on hotel business and could give you a lift."

"It sounds interesting." Kathryn was

ready for something other than the beach. "We'd love to come."

Rafael gave a time then said, "I hear you had visitors this morning. No bother, I hope?"

"Not really!" Kathryn didn't know quite what to say.

"I understand." His voice was sympathetic. "Luis has had a trying time recently and can be a handful. He needs someone older and firmer while Teresa could do with leading her own life a little more."

"I think you're right!"

"It would be better for the boy to be in Madrid where his friends are. But enough of their problems!" Rafael dismissed them. "Have a quiet afternoon!"

"I intend to," Kathryn chuckled.

It seemed fated to be a day of interrupted meals for Olivia arrived half-way through lunch. "I came to collect Luis. Anna said he has gone." She looked around as though doubting the woman's word.

"Teresa took him home," Kathryn confirmed.

"He does so love the beach," Olivia said.

"But not the water." Kathryn poured her visitor a glass of fruit juice.

"It is unfortunate." Olivia seemed displeased over her son's failing. "I have ordered him into the swimming-pool but he just stands and cries."

"He's very young," Kathryn said.

"True." Olivia brightened. "How far can you swim?" A smile accompanied the question to Deborah.

"Four hundred metres."

"Oh!" The unexpected answer took her aback for a moment then she smiled again. "It does not do to push children."

Kathryn bent over her plate to hide her expression. The woman could be as irritating as her son. Anna came to clear the table and Kathryn helped. In the kitchen the older woman jerked a thumb in Olivia's direction and raised an eyebrow. Kathryn spread her hands in a gesture of ignorance.

Olivia appeared in the doorway. "Has Rafael been yet? I assume he comes every day to check the house."

Diplomatically Kathryn said, "You'd better ask Anna."

Olivia didn't seem to get far with the elderly woman who began washing up with an air of indifference.

"I keep telling Rafael he should be more distant with Anna," Olivia said with a snap. "It never does to be on too friendly terms with employees."

A maxim she clearly didn't apply to herself, thought Kathryn with amusement.

Olivia walked to her car. "I thought Rafael would be here and we could have a quiet talk. We had a quarrel the other night and need to make up. I was upset by the whole affair and he can be very stubborn."

Kathryn spent part of the afternoon pondering the woman's parting words. Although it was *absolutely* none of

61

her business she was intrigued by the implied relationship. And where was Señor Santini?

* * *

They were ready in good time on Thursday for the trip to Almeria. Rafael, formal in lightweight suit and pale shirt, drove up in a new estate car with 'Hotel Mediterraneo' neatly lettered on the side. "We go in style today since I'm on hotel business."

"Are you sure we won't be in the way?"

Rafael ushered Deborah into the rear seat. "I'll drop you off, go to the meeting then pick you up again." Inside the car he handed Kathryn an English guide to Almeria including a map. He pencilled a cross at one point. "That's the place I'll meet you."

Rafael had to reverse the long car back to the road. "I'll go the other way so you can see the village. It isn't far out of our way."

We won't go past the hotel either, Kathryn suddenly thought. Was it just another kind gesture on Rafael's part — or didn't he want anyone there to know he had passengers to Almeria?

3

THE old port of Almeria, overlooked by its Arab fortress, was crowded with tourists enjoying the atmosphere of the sun-filled streets. Rafael dropped Kathryn and Deborah at the place he'd marked on the map saying he'd be back in two hours. Deborah didn't normally like wandering round the shops but was intrigued enough by the Spanish ones to enjoy it. They sat in one of the open-air cafés to give her a rest before making their way to the meeting-place.

Rafael arrived on foot. "I thought you'd be loaded with parcels," he greeted. "The shops are tempting."

"Not today," Kathryn returned lightly. At the end of the holiday, when she knew what money was spare, they could shop with the intention of buying.

"Did you see the cathedral?" he

asked. "I left the car there in case you haven't."

"Is that a church!" Kathryn exclaimed ten minutes later. "It looks more like a castle!" The heavy corner towers could only have been constructed with defence in mind.

"The town was often raided by pirates so some kind of protection was needed."

"Real pirates here!" Deborah's imagination was fired by the idea. "Where did they come from?"

"The Barbary states of North Africa," Rafael answered. "There were frequent attacks along the coast."

"I wouldn't have liked that," Deborah shuddered. "You could have got taken away and never seen again."

"Now the area is invaded by thousands of tourists," Kathryn chuckled. "The cathedral probably still needs its thick walls."

"The car's up this road," Rafael told them. "We'll go to the Alcazaba. That really is a castle."

The original Moorish structure had been extended at a later date and linked with another castle, now in ruins, on an adjoining hill. The view over the town and harbour absorbed Kathryn while Rafael took Deborah round part of the fortress.

The Gulf of Almeria had ships moving across it leaving wide spreading wakes on the deep blue surface. The sun was high and Kathryn was glad of the broad brim of her hat. The heat bounced off the walls of the fortress and she looked anxiously for her daughter.

"We've seen as much as we could," Deborah told her mother, "but there's a lot more."

The car was like an oven and Rafael got moving fast so the air streamed through the windows. He branched off the coast road a few miles out of Almeria. "I'm calling to see a friend and his family. I rang to let him know we were coming. His wife's English and loves someone from home to talk to."

Jane Rodise was small, dark, late

twenties and very pregnant. "I can't get up," she laughed. "There's too much of me."

Her husband, Tomas, brought extra chairs on to the patio and dispensed cold drinks.

"Tomas' English is quite good now," Jane explained. "It was non-existent when we first met, like my Spanish."

"How did you meet?" Kathryn asked, taking the glass Tomas handed her.

"Four of us came on holiday to one of the tourist hotels in Benidorm. Tomas was working there as a chef. We wrote to each other for a year while I studied the language furiously at evening classes. Tomas got another job at the Mediterraneo where he met Rafael."

Kathryn looked at the two men deep in conversation. "Is Tomas still at the Mediterraneo?"

"No." Jane shook her head. "He was raised by his grandmother. The old lady is rather frail now. We couldn't leave her on her own any longer. This house is hers. Rafael was marvellous when the position was explained to him. He found Tomas another job in Almeria so he could live here."

The talk shifted to England and Deborah joined in. After an hour Tomas and Rafael went into the house and returned with large trays of food.

"We're picnicking," Jane explained. "You must be hungry after walking the town all morning."

The tinkling of a small bell sounded from within. Tomas went at once and came back pushing an old lady in a wheelchair. Rafael introduced Kathryn and Deborah very formally. "Señora Rodise is nearly eighty and not in the best of health."

Kathryn and the old lady talked between mouthfuls with Rafael translating. At one point Señora Rodise stretched out a lined hand to touch Kathryn's pale hair. "She says you are like a moonbeam."

"More like a ghost!" Kathryn said with a wry grin.

"Señora Rodise also says your

daughter is as pretty as her mother."

Deborah twinkled at the old lady who smiled at her. The little girl beamed and passed her another drink. The meal finished, the talk languished. Señora Rodise nodded off and so did Deborah in an armchair. Jane excused herself saying she had to lie down for an hour.

They left at seven for the journey back. Before they went Señora Rodise sent Tomas to her room. The doll he fetched the old lady gave to Deborah who was speechless.

"We couldn't!" Kathryn turned to Rafael. "It's too expensive."

They had seen flamenco dolls in the shops that morning but this was no factory produced item for the tourist trade. The rufffled silk dress was beautifully hand-stitched and trimmed with lace. Tiny castanets were held in the delicate fingers, the whole thing a work of care and expertise.

"No," Jane denied. "We buy the

dolls in the market and Nan dresses them. It's her only pastime now. Please don't offend her by refusing."

"Thank you." Deborah hugged the doll. "She's lovely."

"*Gracias*," Kathryn said to Señora Rodise. On impulse she kissed the wrinkled cheek. "*Muchas gracias*."

In the car Deborah twirled the doll round, making the dress flare. "Wasn't it kind of Tomas' gran to give me this."

Kathryn smiled at her daughter's enthusiasm. Señora Rodise could not have given a more welcome present.

"Do you have a grandmother, Deborah?" Rafael asked, swinging the car on to the coast road.

She was engrossed in the doll and it was left to Kathryn to say, "She lives in Yorkshire which is some way from us. We don't meet very often."

"That's a pity! You no doubt feel the need of your mother's advice from time to time."

"It's my mother-in-law who's in

70

Yorkshire," Kathryn explained. "My parents are dead."

"Oh!" His quick glance was sympathetic. "You have no-one to support you."

Kathryn laughed. "Makes me sound like a sagging fence!"

"You know what I mean!"

"We have some good friends who fill in for the family we haven't got. We're not alone and helpless."

"Helpless is the last word I would apply to you!" It was spoken with feeling and Kathryn knew he was thinking of their first meeting.

"What about your family, Rafael?" she asked. "Do they live locally?"

He turned off the coast road on to the side one that led to his house. "My sister lives in Switzerland and our aunt in England. When my father died suddenly ten years ago my mother went to live with my sister."

He brought the car down the short drive to the house. Getting out Kathryn thanked him for the trip and the chance of meeting the Rodise family.

"I'll be seeing you," he promised and drove off.

★ ★ ★

"I enjoyed today," Deborah said over supper. "Fancy pirates coming around here." She looked out to the horizon. "It would be very scary!"

Kathryn agreed. "That's why they built strong places like the cathedral and the Alcazaba."

"I like it here," Deborah went on, helping herself to extra food. "It's not a bit like home."

Again Kathryn agreed. Deborah was eating more and was losing the pinched look which had so worried her mother. Earlier reservations about the wisdom of bringing her to Spain had completely disappeared.

The pair of them examined the doll more closely before going to bed. The intricate stitching on the frills of the skirt must have taken many hours.

Señora Rodise had plenty of skill in her old fingers.

Several days later Teresa brought Luis to the beach again. Kathryn's spirits sank at the sight of their disgruntled faces.

"Me holiday today," Teresa scowled. "Now Olivia too busy for Luis. Me no holiday."

She removed skirt and tee-shirt and marched into the water, striking out in a fast crawl indicative of her bad temper. Kathryn sighed to herself. She wished Teresa had taken her black mood somewhere else.

A squabble soon broke out between Deborah and Luis, each shouting in their own language. Kathryn went to break it up, sending her daughter off with the inflatable duck. Holding Luis by the hand she took him near the shelter where he'd left his spade. She mimed building something. Luis wasn't interested. *He* wanted the duck! Kathryn left him to his sulks and joined Deborah in the water. Luis hovered at the water's edge watching with longing eyes. Gradually his envy overcame his fear and he inched forward.

Arriving back flushed and panting Teresa stared disbelievingly at the boy in the sea. As if suddenly aware of his position Luis dashed to the sand and stood wide-eyed.

"Come on, Luis," Deborah called. "Don't be afraid."

He understood the tone if not the words and ventured back with a wary intent. Telling Deborah to stay in the very shallow area Kathryn quietly withdrew. Luis would do better without her.

The long swim had dissipated Teresa's bad temper. She flopped on the sand beside Kathryn with a wide grin containing a touch of admiration. "You good with Luis.

Teresa was a pretty girl with large brown eyes and an attractive figure. Kathryn wished conversation was easier, both with her and the boy.

"Rafael good with Luis," Teresa added. "Everything better after married."

Kathryn was puzzled by the remark. Seeing her expression Teresa said, "Rafael and Olivia marry soon."

It certainly explained Olivia's proprietary attitude towards her manager. "What happened to Luis' father?"

Now it was Teresa who was puzzled. Kathryn tried again. "Where is the father of Luis?"

Teresa turned on to her front. "He not here."

Kathryn stared at the reclining girl. "What do you mean?"

It was too complicated for Teresa to follow and she looked blank. "Rafael and Olivia to marry long time. They . . . " She struggled for the right word then pointed to her finger. "They have ring."

Kathryn's eyes widened. Did she mean there had been an engagement? "What went wrong?"

Teresa shrugged and said, "Olivia marry Jorge Santini. He not here now."

75

She glanced at the position of the sun, called to Luis and departed, the boy protesting loudly.

"I don't like Luis much," Deborah announced, perching on the edge of the other lounger. "He wants everything for himself."

"He's lonely," Kathryn observed in mitigation.

"He's selfish!" her daughter declared.

"Luis is young and has a lot to learn," Kathryn pointed out. "He enjoyed being with you this morning."

"More like work than play," Deborah grumbled. "I hope he doesn't come again."

"Now you are being selfish," her mother censured.

Deborah threw her a dark look. "He's a pain!"

Kathryn tried to keep her face straight but failed. Deborah rolled backwards off the lounger in a fit of laughter. Recovering she suggested they went to eat. "I'm starving."

"It's been so long since breakfast!"

"The sea makes me hungry," Deborah stated.

Rafael rang during lunch. "May I come round later or have you had enough visitors for one day?"

"Bring your own duck!" Kathryn chuckled.

"If Luis is too much," Rafael said on his arrival, "I'll tell Teresa not to bring him while you're here."

Kathryn was tempted. She did find the boy rather wearing. On the other hand she was leaving on Saturday and it wasn't fair to deny Luis access to the beach.

"No," she said at last. "I'll be all right. It's only a few more days and Luis usually behaves after a while."

"A pity you're not here for longer," Rafael commented. "The place really agrees with Deborah. I've never seen such a change in a youngster."

Deborah was on the terrace making the flamenco doll dance on the table. Her skin was tanned and there was an eagerness about the child which

77

Kathryn hadn't seen for ages.

"And you, too," Rafael added. "You're much more relaxed." One finger lightly brushed across her forehead. "All the little worry lines have gone."

"Because the worries have gone." Kathryn lay back in a chair. "Deborah's illness frightened me. Now all is well and the relief is overwhelming." The wide smile appeared, her blue eyes very bright. "Thank you again for lending us your house."

"You are welcome." From the other chair his dark eyes absorbed her. "The house will miss you."

Kathryn had the oddest urge to ask if he would miss her too — and was startled by the wayward thought. A little unnerved by it she rushed into speech. "I'd have thought Señora Santini would have stayed here. It would be convenient for Luis as he likes the beach."

Rafael laughed, the lines crinkling round his eyes and mouth. "This is too simple a dwelling for Olivia. She prefers the suite at the hotel with instant service and constant variety."

Kathryn was amused by his description. "She told me she'd rather be here than in the city."

"She does prefer it here," Rafael agreed, "but not for the sea and sand."

Kathryn recalled Teresa's words that morning. Rafael being here would ensure Olivia did not stay too long.

"Does Luis stay at the hotel as well?" she asked.

"Yes." Rafael stretched his legs out, hands clasped behind his neck. "Olivia's still not decided what to do. She lived with her father for a time before his death but she's since sold the house. She may buy one around here although properties are pricey. Still, her husband made her a generous settlement."

"Husband! But I thought . . . " Kathryn stopped, feeling a fool. After the talk this morning she'd assumed Olivia was a widow like herself.

"I should have said ex-husband.

She and Jorge Santini were recently divorced." There was nothing in his face or voice to hint at his views on the matter.

Cautiously Kathryn said, "A marriage break-up is distressing."

"Luis doesn't like it at the hotel," Rafael said, "so he's difficult to deal with. I hope you can bear with him if he visits here."

"Of course." Kathryn's tone was sympathetic. "He must be lonely without permanent playmates."

"Time Olivia realised it," Rafael concurred.

Deborah came bouncing in. "Let's go for a swim. I'll race you.

"Not me!" Kathryn stayed where she was. "I haven't the energy to race."

"I wouldn't mind a swim," Rafael said. "Let me get changed and I'll come with you." He disappeared into the main bedroom where he had a quantity of clothes.

Kathryn read for a while then went to join them on the beach. Watching from the shelter she marvelled at his patience. He certainly seemed to have the touch in dealing with children. Her daughter was usually reserved with people she'd only recently met but Rafael had been admitted at once to her friendship. She could hear a lot of chatter from Deborah and guessed Rafael was getting details of their life in England which turned out to be true.

"I know everything about your new flat," Rafael revealed, coming under the shelter, "even the cupboard door that wouldn't stay shut."

"I kept walking into it," Kathryn chuckled. "I finally had to put a bolt on it."

Deborah was in the sea again, fair hair slicked down, turning back flips. His gaze on her Rafael said, "Deborah never mentions her father. Doesn't she remember him too well?"

"She never knew him. Colin was killed in a car accident four months before she was born."

Rafael drew a quick breath, eyes

gentle with compassion, though he said nothing.

"The pain has gone only the regrets remain," Kathryn said. "Regret we had so short a time, regret Deborah and Colin never knew each other. Many things really, mainly that my memories are growing dim. One day I'll have none."

"You'll have Deborah," he gently reminded her.

Kathryn roused herself and gave him a bright smile. "How serious we are! Far too much for a sunny day." She changed the subject. "Have you been busy? Time off must be a problem."

He trickled some sand through his fingers. "It's not too bad. I'm up early and I usually do the paperwork in the afternoon. An air-conditioned office is a great help." Rafael built the sand into a small heap, the fine grains sprinkling from his hand. "I hope you don't mind my coming here. I find it very relaxing. Don't hesitate to say if you'd prefer me not to."

"Can't ban you from your own house," she laughed.

"That's not what I meant!" Rafael snapped in sudden irritation. Relenting immediately he apologised. "I'm a bit tired."

"Then stop playing with the sand and put your feet up for a while."

He smiled. "You sound like Anna!" Nevertheless he complied. "The place is restful and so are you."

"Like an old slipper!" Kathryn remarked dryly.

His gaze swept her swim-suited figure with a disconcerting thoroughness. "Not at all like that!"

Off-balance Kathryn felt her colour rise and she looked away. He had no business teasing other women when he was involved with his employer. "What's Olivia doing today?" she inquired.

"I've no idea," he replied with a lazy grin. "She started the day by quarrelling with Teresa and so I've been giving her a wide berth."

"Teresa said." Kathryn vividly recalled other things the girl had said. "Have you known Olivia long?"

Rafael considered for a moment. "It must be fifteen years. Our families were close at that time."

Not him and Olivia specifically? Had she misunderstood Teresa's poor English? The girl had been emphatic about Rafael and her cousin.

On the water Deborah was attempting to stand on the duck's back. She managed it at last, wobbling for several seconds before spread-eagling into the sea, spray glittering against the blue.

"She'll remember this through the winter," Kathryn remarked. "It's turned out to be a wonderful holiday."

"Is it back to the grindstone on Monday?" Rafael's eyes were on the cavorting child.

"No, thank goodness! Being an instructor I have the school holidays so I don't begin work again until the end of August."

His gaze switched to her in a swift

movement. "But that's a month away!"

"One of the good things about my job," Kathryn told him. "Deborah and I are at home together."

About to say more Kathryn saw Rafael wasn't listening. He had a far-away look on his face as if thinking deeply and barely aware of her presence. She lay back on the lounger and watched Deborah's antics.

"I have to go." Rafael was on his feet. "Something I must attend to."

Kathryn stared at his departing back perplexed by his abrupt leaving. To be honest she enjoyed his company and found it hard to believe they'd only met ten days ago.

★ ★ ★

The phone rang as Kathryn was putting Deborah to bed. "I forgot to tell you Jane Rodise called to see if you'd like to visit again before you go home. She can't get about easily otherwise they'd come here."

"I'd like to," Kathryn responded with pleasure.

"On Thursday," he arranged. "I'll come for you."

Deborah was pleased to hear of the invitation and quite willing to go to town to find a small present for the forthcoming baby. It was their first trip to the little town since arriving in Spain. Choosing a present took some time. Finally Deborah selected a wooden pull-along dog which waggled its head as the wheels turned.

It was a relief to leave the bustle of the shops and find a café for a cooling drink. "If we come to Spain again we must learn some more words." Deborah sipped her drink. "Anna has been teaching me a few in the kitchen before you're up."

"Yes, we could." Kathryn didn't want to spoil her daughter's mood by saying it was unlikely they'd come abroad again for years.

"It's lucky Rafael can speak to us," Deborah went on. "We wouldn't have anyone if he didn't."

They walked along by the side of the beach. There was hardly a piece of unoccupied sand, the whole area crowded with shouting, laughing holiday-makers. Several transistors were playing and ball games were in progress.

"What a lot of people!" Deborah goggled.

"And din!" To Kathryn the boisterous clamour made the day seem hotter. An hour here would produce a nagging headache. Once again she felt grateful for Rafael's generosity over the house.

* * *

On Thursday evening Jane Rodise was propped up on a sofa looking rather drawn.

"We won't stay long," Kathryn promised. "You must be worn out."

"Junior should have arrived two days ago," Jane said. "I can hardly wait for it all to be over now."

Tomas handed round some drinks

telling them his grandmother had had a bad day and had gone to bed.

Jane talked about her life in Spain and its differences from England. "My friends told me I was coming to a backward country where you had to boil the water and women were slaves," she recalled with a grin.

"I keep her under my thumb," Tomas said, his brown eyes brimming.

Jane wagged a finger at him. "Your friends said nobody in their right mind would marry an English girl."

Tomas spread his hands. "Insanity runs in my family."

They all laughed, Jane holding one hand to her aching side. "English girls have a terrible reputation along the coast so it wasn't surprising Tomas' friends tried to talk him out of it."

"Now I recommend them all to have an English wife. They are the best."

"You haven't had a Spanish one so you can't compare," Rafael said with a straight face.

"No." Tomas jabbed a knowing

finger at him. "And you haven't had a wife of any kind so you can't give an opinion at all."

"I'm working on it," Rafael protested, leaning back in his chair with a satisfied air.

Tomas said something in Spanish and the other two laughed. Nobody translated for Kathryn and she was left guessing at Tomas' riposte to Rafael's obvious reference to Olivia. The Rodise house was a lot like the one in which they were staying with high ceilings and an outside space used as an extension to the living-area. Kathryn couldn't see Olivia settling for such a place and wondered how Rafael was going to house his new wife.

Kathryn gave Jane her address before their departure an hour later. "Please let me know about the baby. Deborah and I have enjoyed meeting you and hope everything goes well."

"Tomas and Jane are a lovely couple," she remarked on the way back. "They seem to fit together."

89

"It was five years before they married so nobody can accuse them of rushing headlong into it," he said.

"Marrying quickly isn't always a failure." Kathryn thought of her own wedding taking place six months after she'd met Colin. How would their marriage have fared?

"Maybe not," Rafael allowed, "but you have to be really sure of yourself and the other person before making such a commitment after so short a time."

"Yes," Kathryn agreed, "though there can be quite a difference between knowing your own feelings and being certain of the other person's."

"Amen to that!" Rafael said with fervour, driving through the town.

Kathryn hadn't got used to the late hours kept by the Spanish. Vaguely studying the groups talking and drinking in the open-air cafés, she sympathised with the man beside her. Events had not been smooth for him. Pity Olivia wasn't more worthy of him!

Enough of that, Kathryn chided herself. Just because you don't like her doesn't mean she won't make a good wife for Rafael.

At the house Kathryn helped her sleepy daughter from the car and put her to bed. Returning to the living-room she was surprised to find Rafael still there, hands in pockets, gazing through the large windows at the moon-dappled sea. He turned and said, "Sit down, Kathryn. I want to talk to you."

His expression was unusually serious and reminded her of the day they'd met. Rafael took the chair opposite and was silent for a moment as though considering his next words with care. "You said you didn't return to work until the end of August. Does that mean you are free for the whole of the month?"

"Yes." Kathryn was baffled by his question, speculating on the reason behind it.

"Since there's no need for you to go

home on Saturday, why don't you stay longer?"

For a space Kathryn could do nothing except stare, the suggestion being the last thing she'd expected. Then, "I couldn't," she rejected.

"Why not?" The dark eyes were very intent.

"It isn't possible."

"Why ever not?" he persisted.

Kathryn twisted her wedding ring round and round, not looking at him. "The truth is I can't afford to stay any longer." She lifted her head and smiled ruefully. "Thank you for asking."

Rafael moved to the edge of his seat. "You haven't had time to consider this fully but I have. Your flight is paid for whether you go on Saturday or the end of the month."

"I couldn't occupy your house for another four weeks," Kathryn protested. "It wouldn't be right."

"I'm offering it to you," Rafael insisted. "Anna comes to clean no matter who's here and she says you are a very tidy lady. The hotel you were to stay in let your room so you're due for a refund. You won't get it yet but I'll keep it to cover the cost of your being here."

"It won't be enough!" Kathryn found another problem. "The hotel won't refund the full amount."

Rafael soon disposed of that quibble. "It wouldn't cover hotel accommodation but for here it will do."

Kathryn chewed her bottom lip torn by indecision and anxiety.

"Is there someone expecting you at home?" Rafael asked in an expressionless tone.

"My neighbour is keeping an eye on the flat. She looks in every day for me."

"There's no reason for you not to stay on." His voice became more persuasive. "Think what a few extra weeks would do for Deborah."

It was Deborah who was absorbing most of her mother's thoughts. For her sake Kathryn knew she should seize this opportunity. Yet she hesitated, her eyes troubled. For all her liking for Rafael she couldn't begin to understand him.

"Do you want to sleep on it?" Rafael's question brought Kathryn from her brief abstraction. "You could discuss it with Deborah then give me a ring."

Kathryn knew exactly what her daughter's reaction would be. She pushed away the doubts. "If you are absolutely certain you don't mind then we'll stay."

"Good." There was a look of satisfaction on his lean face. "I will see to the air tickets. You'll be able to see Jane's baby after all."

Kathryn laughed and fetched the return part of their airline ticket. Rafael tucked it into an inside pocket and headed for the door.

The sky was clear and full of stars. A stillness shadowed this side of the incline and Kathryn felt a peaceful contentment to be part of the lovely night.

"Good night, Kathryn." Totally out of the blue Rafael leaned down and kissed her quickly.

Peace and contentment fled before the brief contact. The car pulled away, the brake lights flashing as it turned on to the road. The sound of it died in the still air as Kathryn remained rooted to the drive.

Rafael's action had raised the qualms so firmly ignored. What game was he playing? And why? Kathryn gazed unseeingly into the night. Had she let herself in for more than she'd bargained?

Don't be a fool, she admonished herself. Don't read more into a casual gesture than was really there. She could trust Rafael. Couldn't she?

4

IN the cool of the misty morning Kathryn's doubts over the wisdom of accepting Rafael's offer seemed groundless. She thought it best to say nothing to her daughter in case the ticket could not be changed.

Anna arrived at her usual time bringing a note written in English. "Please come down to the village tonight with your little girl. There is a party and I would like you to come."

"*Gracias*, Anna." Kathryn read the note to Deborah. "*Si*, we'll come."

Deborah nodded vigorously to make sure Anna understood and was delighted with the beam on her face.

"You look nice," Deborah told her mother that evening.

"Thank you, love." Kathryn gave a final flick to her hair and said she was ready. The dark blue dress had a ruched bodice and straps that tied on each shoulder. It was safe for her to wear now that the sting had gone from the sun.

Deborah skipped up the drive while Kathryn locked the door. Her pink dress showed she'd tanned beautifully during their time here. The sky was fading into twilight, the sun low on the hazy horizon. Deborah thought it exciting to be going out at a time she was normally in bed.

They heard the music before they came round the last bend. Deborah had been hoping for flamenco dancers like her doll though her mother had said it was unlikely. Kathryn was proved right. In dresses and shirts, the villagers were dancing in the square to disco music.

"Señora Morris?" A young man detached himself from the crowd. "I am Andres, Anna's grandson." He led them round the side of the small square to where Anna was sitting at a table with several other people. Andres beckoned a girl to his side. "This is Dorotea who has agreed to marry me. Everybody helps us to celebrate," he added with a wave at the crowded square.

It seemed to Kathryn that everyone was indeed there. Tables and chairs were set out round the little square leaving the centre clear for dancing. In spite of the language difficulty Kathryn and Deborah were made welcome, chairs and drinks appearing for them.

Later Andres and Dorotea performed a lively *paso doble* to the accompaniment of calls and handclaps from the audience. It was near two o'clock when Kathryn saw Rafael on the other side of the square making his way in their direction. Everybody knew him. There were handshakes and greetings all the way to the table.

"Sampling the local hospitality?" He sank into the chair next to her.

"Anna invited us," Kathryn informed him. "Her grandson got engaged."

"Yes, I know." He tapped his fingers on the table in time to the music. "Are you enjoying yourself?"

"Very much. Please thank Anna for me."

Rafael shot some Spanish across the table at Anna who leaned forward and patted Kathryn's hand.

"You're well known here," Kathryn said to him. "Are you a frequent visitor?"

"My grandmother was from this village." He stood up. "Come and dance."

They joined the smiling crowd, swaying and turning to music issuing from the loudspeakers set at each end of the square. Rafael knew all the names. Laughing remarks were tossed at him often accompanied by a bright-eyed glance at Kathryn. The square cleared to allow the engaged couple another solo dance. Rafael had his arm casually round Kathryn's shoulders occasionally calling out in Spanish to the dancing couple. Kathryn felt very much at home, relaxed and happy.

At their table Rafael said, "Does

all this remind you of your own engagement and wedding?" He poured himself a glass of wine from the bottle Anna pushed over.

"Not really," Kathryn replied. "It was much quieter than this."

"How did you meet your husband?"

"He was a student at the Polytechnic and came to a local dance with some friends. We married six months later."

"And never had the chance to find out if 'young love' would have lasted!" A decided edge on Rafael's voice brought Kathryn's head round, the blue eyes inquiring. "I'm not in favour of early marriages." There was no mistaking the bitter underlay to his words. "The errors that are committed before the people involved have enough sense and experience to avoid them!"

"Some people," Kathryn emphasised, "try so hard to avoid errors they avoid everything and end up with no life at all."

Rafael put his elbows on the table. "Which sort are you?" he questioned,

100

the hardness still there.

"I'm a bit of both," Kathryn answered after due consideration. "A well-rounded character!"

"Well-rounded everywhere!" As on the beach his scrutiny took in all the details. "You look about twenty. Nobody would guess you had a daughter of Deborah's age."

"Thank you," Kathryn murmured not losing her poise this time. "Is this the Spanish charm I've heard about!"

"No," he returned, "Spanish truth!"

Andres came to fetch his grandmother for a dance and was assured by Kathryn she was having a good time. "He's walking on air."

"But what of tomorrow when all goes sour!"

"It probably won't, you cynic!" She shot him a provoking look. "Anyway not everyone wants to wait until they're middle-aged."

"Ouch!" He poured more wine for them.

She recalled his earlier words. "You

must have gathered enough sense and experience by now."

Rafael leaned forward so he was much closer. "I have and I've decided the random selection method of choosing a wife is too inefficient. I'm thinking of using business practice instead."

Kathryn put her chin on one hand. "Tell me more."

"When there's a vacancy at the hotel I look round for a suitable candidate to fill it. It seems a good way of finding a wife."

"Have you located many candidates for the wife vacancy yet?"

"I don't want to boast but I'm not without my admirers." Rafael couldn't keep back a grin.

Kathryn kept her face straight. "Your natural modesty probably attracts them."

"What about you?" He raised his glass in silent salute. "You'd be ideal."

She was savouring the banter. "Are you sure?"

"You are level-headed and practical as well as being past the age of flightiness. I know you're hard-working and responsible. What more could I want?"

Their eyes held — and suddenly there was no joke at all! Instead a searching, a reaching-out that Kathryn couldn't understand. It left her breathless and uncertain.

Leaning back from him she said in a voice that shook, "I already have a job so I won't be applying for your vacancy."

Sharply he rebuked, "Marriage isn't a job!"

"I know that better than you!" Kathryn's voice was very low. "Perhaps you should get some more sense before you start wife-hunting. You sound as though you could make quite a mistake."

"Which you didn't!" The grimness was back around his mouth.

"That's impossible to answer." Kathryn looked at him honestly. "I loved Colin enough to want to spend the rest of my life with him. It wasn't to be but one thing is certain. I wouldn't remarry unless I felt the same way again."

Anna's smiling return broke the sombre atmosphere at the table. In rapid Spanish she urged them to dance once more. They circled in silence each deep in their own thoughts. Kathryn stifled a yawn and reproached herself for a lack of stamina.

"Past your bedtime." Rafael was regarding her with a hard-to-read expression.

"What about you? At least I haven't been to work."

In a swift lightening of his mood he said, "I'm a man of iron."

"Your modesty is showing again," she chuckled and, harmony restored, he gathered her closer to dance in warm companionship for a while.

"Deborah and I must be going," Kathryn said to him at the end of the music. "Tell Anna we've enjoyed it."

"You can come again," he disclosed

and pulled an airline envelope from his pocket.

Kathryn gazed at the changed ticket. "You did it!"

"It was nothing," Rafael dismissed. He told Anna of the new arrangement and she was delighted.

"I'll tell Deborah in the morning." Kathryn looked to where her daughter was sitting with some children. She ambled over when called.

"I'll run you home." Rafael stood up. "Come on, little one." With no effort he picked Deborah up and let her rest on him. With a final word to Anna they left, farewells echoing in the still crowded square.

"How long will this go on?" Kathryn took a last look at the revellers.

"Some time yet." Rafael directed her to the car. "We keep late hours in Spain."

"Will they have to work tomorrow?"

Rafael unlocked the doors. "Most of the people here are employed in hotels along the coast. The more hardy souls

105

will go straight from the celebration to work."

"No wonder the country shuts down in the afternoon," Kathryn commented, getting into the front passenger seat. "It seems a strange way to live. I doubt whether I could get used to it."

Rafael reached for the ignition. "You could if you really wanted to."

It was difficult to see each other clearly so Kathryn couldn't get a good look at his face. She hoped he hadn't believed she was being critical. His tone had been rather stiff. Arriving at the house Rafael saw them inside, said good-bye with a ruffle of Deborah's hair and drove off into the velvet night.

In the morning instead of returning home with the rest of their party, Kathryn and Deborah had a lie-in and a leisurely breakfast. The conversation with Rafael kept re-occurring. Kathryn knew it had all been a joke yet it had an upsetting effect on her. If Teresa had her facts right Rafael had cause to believe 'young love' was not long-lasting. What had terminated the engagement? How much had Rafael been hurt by Olivia marrying somebody else?

And why am I bothered whether he was or not? Kathryn spent a fair amount of time on that point before finally conceding she was attracted to him in a way she hadn't been to any man since her husband. Worried by this, she told herself being away from home in such a lovely place, with the sunshine and different customs, had all contributed to her reaction. If she'd met Rafael on a wet day in England she'd probably not have given him a second glance.

Kathryn had not convinced herself this was entirely true when she went to bed that night.

★ ★ ★

She was surprised by Anna arriving the following morning for she didn't normally come on Sundays. The elderly

Spaniard clattered about the kitchen far from her usual pleasant self. Kathryn and Deborah stayed out of her way unable to think of a reason for Anna's anger.

The reason came half an hour later bringing Luis. In an exquisite linen two-piece Olivia Santini looked every inch the wealthy woman of fashion she was. Delicate filigree jewellery encircled her neck and wrist whilst an assortment of rings decorated her long fingers. She walked through to the living-room. "I have a favour to ask. Really it is a favour for Rafael."

Kathryn followed her. "What is it?"

"I had a call from an old friend yesterday saying she and her husband would be in Almeria for a couple of days. We haven't seen each other for some time and we agreed to spend today together. Naturally Rafael is accompanying me."

Naturally! thought Kathryn.

"I promised Teresa faithfully she could have the day off so I could not expect her to cancel her plans at such short notice then I thought of you," Olivia's smile was a little lacking in real warmth. "Could you have Luis until we return?"

"There's no-one at the hotel?" Kathryn inquired without much hope.

"Not as good with him as you." The smile widened. "Luis told me he went into the water. You have a way with him and Anna agreed to come to help."

She waited expectantly. Kathryn was not pleased with the request and, from her attitude, neither was Anna. She began to frame a tactful refusal.

"I know you would want to help Rafael," Olivia went on, indicating the room with a wide sweep of her hand. "Letting you stay on was an act of great unselfishness on his part. I do not want him to have the bother of Luis at the moment. Rafael does not understand him but then men rarely have any interest in other people's children, do they!"

Kathryn felt she was being backed into a corner.

"Until everything is settled between Rafael and me I prefer not to have him upset." Strange how coy so sophisticated a woman could look!

Kathryn gave way to her boundless curiosity. "Settled?"

Olivia fiddled with the strap of her bag. "It will not go any further, I know. Rafael and I have always been close and now my divorce is finalised . . . " She left the sentence hanging.

Kathryn was able to supply the ending. Rafael's 'young love' had come back to him.

"You will have Luis for us, please." Olivia stood up. "After Rafael spent most of Thursday getting your ticket changed, I felt sure you would want to repay him." Her tone indicated disapproval of his action.

Put like that there was nothing Kathryn could do except agree although it was clear she was not in for an easy day. With Luis mutinous at being left,

Deborah not wanting to play with him, Anna in a bad mood and her own reluctance, the omens were not good.

The first part of the morning dragged fraying Kathryn's usually even temper. Even when it was quite obvious what she meant Luis pretended not to understand. Kathryn felt if she heard *no entiendo* once more she'd scream. To her credit Deborah made every effort to help and eventually got Luis into a better frame of mind. From then on it was more pleasant.

Kathryn's thoughts dwelt on the boy and his mother. She had every sympathy for the youngster, realising how emotionally difficult his life must be. As for Olivia, Kathryn reserved judgement, knowing her antipathy to the woman would probably warp her verdict. The feeling seemed mutual. Olivia was annoyed by the prolonging of their stay at Rafael's house and Kathryn wondered if he'd offered without telling her he was doing so.

No, that wasn't true! Olivia had

known of his altering the ticket on Thursday so she could have stopped him if . . . ! Kathryn frowned. Rafael couldn't have exchanged it on Thursday because she'd only agreed to stay that evening. Olivia must have meant Friday.

Her attention went back to Luis. He was still inclined to be possessive over the inflatable duck but Deborah was especially forbearing so there were no quarrels. Occasionally Kathryn thought she could see glimpses of the boy Luis really was.

Around half-past one she brought the two children up from the beach for something to eat. A much brighter Anna was waiting, having set the terrace table ready.

Rafael rang during the meal. "I must apologise. I've only just learned Olivia has left Luis with you. How are you managing?"

"Not too badly," Kathryn answered. "I don't really mind having him if it helps you out."

"He could well have stayed at the hotel with me except Olivia insisted on my driving her today." He sounded exasperated.

"Anna and I are fine," Kathryn assured him. "Have a good time."

"I rang a little earlier when Olivia told me about Luis. Anna can only stay a bit longer. Will you be all right on your own? We'll be back as soon as I can get Olivia away."

"It's hotter than ever," Kathryn said, "so we'll be in the house for the afternoon. There shouldn't be any problems."

She'd put the phone down before one occurred to her. It took a lot of miming and drawing to get Anna to understand then she gave Luis his orders. He was not to leave the house without Kathryn. Luis thrust out his bottom lip and muttered at Anna. She did a quick sketch of a duck floating on the sea. Much alarmed Kathryn shook her head. Luis received a stern lecture from Anna which deflated him completely.

He went into a sulk, throwing himself in a chair and refusing to help clear the table.

The others left him alone. Anna went shortly afterwards shaking her head over the boy. Deborah retired to the bedroom to read on her bed. Kathryn sat in the living-room ignoring the sullen child. Gradually her eyelids drooped and she let the book close. Turning her head to one side Kathryn fell asleep.

* * *

"Mum! Wake up, Mum!" An urgent hand shook Kathryn by the shoulder. "Wake up!"

She blinked, sitting upright and pushing back her hair. "What's the matter?"

Deborah's face was pale with fright. "It's Luis! Come and look." She pulled at her mother.

Shaking off the last remnants of sleep Kathryn stood up to follow her rushing daughter to the window. Her gaze swept the section of beach visible at this angle. Where was the tiresome child? A flash of red caught her attention and she gasped aloud. Luis, on the duck, was some distance out on the water.

For a long moment Kathryn froze, the shock numbing her mind then her wits returned and she was across the room and on to the terrace. Luis was around three hundred yards from the shore. He must have left the house soon after she'd dropped asleep.

Help! She had to have help! But where! The phone was no use. If she ran to the hotel a boat could go providing they had one! This was not the time to discover they hadn't. Kathryn raced for the steps, skipping down them with desperate haste, Deborah at her heels. At the water's edge she threw off her dress.

"Don't go, Mum!" Deborah was full of fear. "It's too far! Please don't go."

"No, love." Kathryn bent down in front of her frightened daughter. "I can make it and I have to go." Striving for a calm tone she unstrapped her watch and gave it to Deborah. "Take this to the bedroom and then bring me a towel."

It would stop Deborah having to see Kathryn wade into the water and begin the long haul out to the drifting child. The breeze, so welcome this morning, was taking the inflatable away from the shore. Deborah had seen the boy just in time. Kathryn estimated it was narrowly within her ability to fetch him.

She settled to the steady rhythm needed to reach the boy and yet conserve energy for the much harder return journey. Thank goodness for the garish red of the duck. She'd never have kept track of Luis otherwise. Even so she couldn't always spot the bobbing object on the swell of the water.

Overhead the sun, searing in its intensity, flayed the sea and land alike. Kathryn could feel its heat on her unprotected shoulders and back, the sensitive skin beginning to tingle. Resolutely she turned her attention away from burning and focused on getting the maximum length on her strokes. She could complete a mile with ease only this wasn't the flat calm of the local baths where the dead water and ideal conditions produced long distances in fast times. The swell meant Kathryn had to deal with the up-and-down motion, an uplift occasionally slapping into her face.

She was close now, the child in her view all the time. Kathryn stopped a couple of yards away from him, treading water and breathing heavily. Luis was rigid with terror, clinging to the duck's neck with all his strength. He'd gone past crying, drained of everything. Any attempt to remove the boy from the inflatable would galvanise him into a threshing panic Kathryn couldn't hope to control.

Aware of the potential danger Kathryn inched forward, talking in a soothing way until she could touch the duck.

Round its neck was the cord Deborah used to pull it through the water. She'd have to tow Luis back. For a moment Kathryn's courage failed. It was too far! Too hard! Too much!

She looked at the boy's set face, the staring eyes, the blank gaze. Then Luis blinked and mumbled, "Mama!"

The strength rose in Kathryn and she was ready for the return. "Hold on," she urged. "Here we go!"

A hundred yards and her shoulders were screaming. Swimming one-armed was difficult at any time. Towing the loaded inflatable proved a nightmare. Kathryn kept changing her hands then turned over and tried backstroke. The sun dazzled into her face making her eyes smart and run. "Keep going. It can't be far!"

Time evaporated into a blaze of sea and sky merging to form a barrier to her progress, chaining her legs and deadening her arms. Mind wandering she fancied she was alone, the last person ever to exist. Why bother with the shore? Here was more restful!

The wave was small but Kathryn was submerged for the first time. Horror shot through her, piercing the mental lethargy, alerting her to a danger greater than physical weariness. Kathryn took hold of herself, sighted up on the house and struck out with new vigour. With painful slowness the house grew. Through misted vision Kathryn could distinguish movement on the beach, hear distant shouting and a much nearer splashing. With muscular strokes someone was powering towards them at a formidable speed.

"Kathryn!" Rafael's face was blurred but his voice reached her with a blessed clarity.

The cord was unwound from her hand and she was free to labour the last thirty yards to the beach, floundering into the shallows before crawling on to the sand. Gasping, sides heaving, a burning, aching mass of pain and fatigue, Kathryn crouched on all fours incapable of further movement.

"Mum!" Deborah was there, tears streaking her worried face. "I thought you wouldn't come back."

Kathryn forced herself back on her heels. "I told you I could make it," she whispered.

Beyond her daughter Kathryn could see Olivia comforting Luis. The boy had his arms round her waist crying noisily, oblivious to the outpouring of endearments above his head. Rafael was removing a dripping shirt having gone into the water dressed except for his shoes. The pale trousers stuck in clinging folds to his legs. Dropping the shirt he came and bent over Kathryn. "How do you feel?"

He helped her upright. She swayed slightly and his grip strengthened. Kathryn shivered and shook, her muscles quivering in silent agony. The water dribbled down her body and on to the sand, drying rapidly in the heated grains.

"How far did you go? Deborah said you'd been gone for ages." Rafael's urgent tone caused Kathryn to open her eyes. "Are you all right?"

"Why bother with her?" Olivia rasped, coming nearer. "She has been totally uncaring and irresponsible. Risking my son's life! He almost drowned through your carelessness!"

"It isn't true," Kathryn defended, taking the towel and wrapping it round her shaking body.

"You're not fit to be with children." Olivia's tirade continued. "I feel sick over this."

"Calm down and let's go up to the house." Rafael's low tone carried a lot of firmness.

"My son nearly died!" Olivia shouted. Luis renewed his crying at her raised voice. "She is thoroughly untrustworthy and a menace to us all."

Kathryn recoiled before the woman's venom.

"Olivia!" Rafael put a hand on her arm. "Don't go on." He changed to Spanish, his tone becoming softer.

Olivia replied in the same language

then she turned her face to his shoulder and burst into tears. The sight was too much for Luis who howled with increased force. Rafael put his arms round the crying woman.

Deborah started sniffing and Kathryn gave up any idea of explanations. All she wanted was the peace of her bedroom. Collecting her discarded dress she took Deborah's hand and trudged across the sand.

At the bottom of the steps Rafael caught up with them. "Let me help you."

Kathryn pushed his hand away. "Go back to your lady-love and the next time you want to go gadding off together, make other provision for the boy!"

The blaze of fury on his face barely registered with Kathryn. She began the ascent, each step seeming like three. Deborah had to help her on the last few. In the bedroom Kathryn removed the soaking bra and pants and put on a cotton wrap. The bed was tempting but there was something else first.

She knew she'd pay dearly for the long exposure to the merciless sun. Trying to lessen the damage was her first priority.

Rafael was crossing the living-room as Kathryn emerged from the bedroom. "I don't need your help," she flared before he could open his mouth.

"It is my house," he reminded in a hard voice. "I can change into dry clothes."

Kathryn brushed past him into the bathroom. Running the bath with cold water she stepped in. Using a sponge she ran the water over her face and body, hoping to check the blistering. Kathryn recognised the seriousness of her condition.

Back in the bedroom she smoothed lotion on to her face then asked Deborah to do her back. The effects of the burning were already painful and would get worse. "Has everyone gone?"

"Yes, when you were in the bathroom."

Kathryn stood up, pulling the wrap into place. In the kitchen she bolted the door then did the same with the terrace one. "I've got to go to bed, Deborah," she told her daughter. "I don't feel at all well. You are not to let anybody in while I'm asleep."

"I won't!" Deborah gave her word.

"No matter who it is!" Kathryn insisted.

She couldn't face anyone, refusing to admit there was only one person she didn't want to encounter again that day. Long after she was in bed, the lengthy hours passing into darkness, the sleep coming and going, not giving her true rest, the clearest image she retained was that of Rafael holding Olivia, their heads close together unmindful of onlookers.

5

ILL as she felt, Kathryn dragged her aching self from the house early the next morning.

"Where are we going?" Deborah was confused by her mother's behaviour.

"Town," Kathryn answered. "I have business there."

"Who with?" Standing by the side of the main road waiting for the bus, Deborah eyed Kathryn anxiously.

"I've forgotten her name but I want to be sure to catch her. That's why we have to go early."

They reached the Christoval to find the tour courier at breakfast. She couldn't remember them until Kathryn added a few words of explanation to her introduction. She produced the airline ticket from her bag. "Could you change this for me."

The courier was reluctant to take it.

"It's very difficult to alter flights at this time of year."

The woman was gone half an hour during which Kathryn strove to ignore the hammers beating in her head and the increasing sting of the sunburn. She'd slept badly, twisting and turning in an effort to find a cool place in the bed. At one stage she thought she heard the phone, at another, voices. She sat in moody silence until the courier's return.

"I'm sorry, Mrs. Morris. All the flights are full."

Kathryn stopped for a drink and two headache tablets before going to catch the bus. They had a longish wait and the sun was high when they got off. The perspiration broke out on Kathryn aggravating the sunburn with cruel intensity. She toiled up the last incline past the hotel, breathing a sigh of relief at the top. Thankfully Kathryn turned into the drive — then stopped dead. Olivia's gleaming car stood by the house! Willingly Kathryn could have fled from her unwelcome visitor.

Olivia was her usual well-dressed self although she seemed strained around the eyes. She stood up when she saw Kathryn. Luis was huddled in a chair looking extremely unhappy.

"Good morning, Señora Morris. We came first thing but unfortunately missed you. I decided to wait because there are things that need to be said."

Kathryn put her bag down. Not another row, she silently pleaded.

"I wish to apologise for yesterday," Olivia said. "I now know it was Luis' fault and not yours. Last night Rafael got the truth from him."

"I see!" Kathryn sank into a chair. She took off the hat and ran unsteady fingers through her damp hair.

Olivia resumed her seat. "When Rafael and I arrived here we saw you and Luis out at sea. We thought it was just a game and came down to the beach. Your daughter was in a distressed state. She said you'd gone after Luis. She kept crying over and over you must have drowned."

She pulled a handkerchief from her bag and blew her nose. "You can imagine the shock it was! Rafael was marvellous. He went in at once to help. After getting Luis back safely I am afraid I went to pieces."

"It was understandable!" Kathryn could afford to be generous in the face of the other woman's remorse.

"I was beside myself with fright. Luis cried for ages afterwards. It was only much later Rafael was able to question him. I thought he was being too hard on Luis but in the end Rafael was right." Olivia sent a forbidding look in her son's direction and he huddled deeper into the chair. She beckoned him and Luis uneasily stood up.

Luis reached for a large bouquet lying on the side table. He gave the flowers to Kathryn. "*Gracias*, Señora." His voice was low, the dark eyes full of tears. Suddenly he threw his arms around her neck. Some faltering Spanish came out in which Kathryn distinguished 'muchas gracias' several times.

"Tell him it's all right now," she requested his mother. "He won't be so silly again."

Olivia mopped Luis' face and made him blow his nose vigorously. "I must also thank you. My son's foolishness could easily have turned to disaster. Please accept this as a small measure of my gratitude." She handed Kathryn a packet with a smile still containing a vestige of shock. "We will leave now. I expect you are in need of rest after yesterday."

Kathryn unwrapped the packet to find a large silk scarf, hand-painted in shades of blue. It was twined through a scarf ring of softly gleaming filigree. Kathryn put it to one side to admire at another time. At the moment she felt too sore and tired to want to do anything other than return to bed.

Wearily going to the bedroom Kathryn tossed hat and glasses on to a chair then removed the clogged make-up. She studied her red and swollen face in the mirror.

A step came from behind her and Rafael walked into the room. "Where the hell have you been?" he demanded.

Kathryn swung round with a gasp at his entrance.

If anything his anger increased. "Look at you!" He crossed to stand in front of her. "You're a fool to be out in that condition!"

"Stop shouting at me!" Kathryn was annoyed at the tremble in her voice. "Go away!"

With a sound of annoyance he turned away and pulled down the bedcover. "Take everything off and get into bed." Kathryn opened her mouth to refuse. "And if you haven't done it by the time I come back, I'll strip you myself!"

The purpose in Rafael's tone had Kathryn unbuttoning before he reached the door. The cotton sheets were cool to her heated skin, her body relaxing even if her mind didn't.

Rafael came back without bothering to knock. He brought a jug of fruit juice and a glass which he placed on the bedside table. Picking up the sunburn lotion he said, "Turn over."

Kathryn, who had the sheet up to her chin, was about to argue, saw his expression and carefully eased on to her stomach. The lotion was gently applied with a pad of cottonwool. The comfort almost outweighed the embarrassment Kathryn felt.

Finishing Rafael ordered, "You stay in bed for a while. I'll take Deborah up to the hotel and bring her back this evening. You have a rest." He was gone without giving her chance to object to this arranging of her day.

She was composing a speech designed to convey exactly what she thought of such high-handed behaviour when she fell asleep.

It was late afternoon, the sun pouring heat on to the silent house, when Kathryn drowsily came awake. The nagging headache was gone and so was a lot of muscular stiffness. She got out of bed to inspect herself in the mirror. The sunburn was the same although a little of the painful stinging had subsided. Pouring some of the fruit juice, she went through to the kitchen to find something to eat. She'd felt too ill to have breakfast.

Rafael brought Deborah back around nine. "How are you, Mum?" she asked at once. "You were very poorly this morning."

"A lot better," Kathryn replied.

"You still look awful!" she observed with a childhood candour which made her mother smile and considerably lightened Rafael's serious expression.

Deborah regaled her mother with her day at the hotel. Kathryn encouraged the talk hoping Rafael would leave before her daughter went to bed. She didn't wish to be alone with him, not after recognising how aware of him she was, and knowing he belonged to someone else. Finally Deborah ran out of words, yawned and said she was ready for bed. Kathryn went with her taking as long as possible before returning to the living-room.

"I'll make a drink." Rafael seemed in no hurry to leave and Kathryn went into the kitchen with the feeling the evening was far from over.

"Thank you for looking after Deborah." She placed the tray on the table, handed Rafael a coffee and sat down with her own. "She seems to have enjoyed herself."

"She's recovered well from the fright." The sombre expression was back. "How about you?"

Kathryn drank some of her coffee. "I'm fine."

"You nearly weren't! How far did you go?"

"About three hundreds yards."

His cup was banged on to its saucer with a muttered exclamation in Spanish. Getting up he paced the room for a minute or two. Kathryn concentrated on her drink and watched his movements out of the corner of her eye.

"You could have drowned!" Rafael stopped by her chair. "I suppose you didn't consider that!"

Kathryn looked up at the dark, unreadable face above her. "As a matter of fact I did! Any further and nothing would have persuaded me to try to fetch him."

"Really!"

The sceptical tone needled Kathryn. She stood up to face him. "Let me assure you I have no time for futile heroic gestures. I would not endanger my life for the sake of someone who cannot or will not obey orders, even if he is only six!" Her blue eyes regarded him gravely. "I weighed the risk before going in. Remember, I left my main responsibility crying on the beach. I was grateful for your help at the end but I would have accomplished it on my own."

His face broke into a reluctant smile. "I'm sure of it! You are a remarkable woman."

Kathryn smiled back. "No, just a practical one."

She poured more coffee and they sat again. Kathryn felt more relaxed. "Luis was very subdued this morning. Did you give him a hard time?"

"Certainly not!" Rafael denied. "I wanted the truth and in the end I got it."

She couldn't really see him being too hard on the boy merely determined.

"And speaking of the truth," Rafael gave her an old-fashioned look, "Olivia and I were not 'gadding about' yesterday. She asked me to drive her to see some friends in Almeria then expected me to stop."

"Sorry about that!" Kathryn's tone was rueful. "I got rather wound up and let fly."

He didn't look entirely convinced. "Also Olivia is not my 'lady love' as you so quaintly phrased it."

"Teresa said something about you being engaged." Kathryn spoke without stopping to think.

"Years ago we were!" The exasperation showed. "It was broken off and Olivia married someone else. Now, through circumstances, we happen to work together."

Very carefully Kathryn said, "I got the impression there was more to it than that."

"Olivia gives the impression there's more to everything than there is. With her flair for the dramatic she should be on the stage."

Rafael did not belong to Olivia! The Spanish woman had been spinning daydreams. You be careful you don't start doing the same! The stern mental warning kept Kathryn from reading too much into Rafael's explanation although it made her feel a lot more cheerful.

"Luis is going back to Madrid to spend some time with Olivia's aunt," Rafael remarked. "She's taking him tomorrow."

"It'll be quiet without them."

"Quieter still if you change your air ticket!"

Dear Deborah! Kathryn might have known she'd tell him. "Yesterday turned everything sour."

"Yesterday was an exceptional day. You won't let it stampede you into anything rash."

"Wanting to go home isn't rash," Kathryn protested.

"For the wrong reason it is," Rafael pointed out. "Don't let it upset you into altering your plans."

Kathryn leaned against the open door and stared out to sea. The sun had gone leaving its warmth in the soft night air.

"You know you are welcome here." Rafael was right behind her.

"Kathryn glanced over her shoulder. "Maybe I did change my mind in too much of a hurry."

"You'll stay." He was pleased by her decision. "I'll take Deborah to the hotel tomorrow again. Why don't you come, too?"

"My lobster face is staying out of sight for a day or two," Kathryn said with deep feeling.

"Be sure to treat it again before you go to bed," he told her, "and the rest of you. I'd be glad to help if you need it."

In haste Kathryn refused. "I won't trouble you."

His voice deepened to a teasing note. "It's no trouble!"

She was thankful for the sunburn for it hid the wash of colour rising under her skin. "I'll manage!"

★ ★ ★

The week that followed was a mixed one for Kathryn. Burnt skin peeled, the irritation giving her a couple of restless nights. Rafael came every morning to check her progress, taking Deborah back with him most days to play with some English children who were guests there.

Kathryn was grateful for his thoughtfulness and for the total rest he was affording her. Rafael was confirmed as number one favourite with Deborah. Her talk was full of him and 'Rafael says' became the clincher in any discussion.

On the first day Kathryn ventured on to the beach Deborah stayed with her, constructing tracks in the sand for the wooden train. The sunburn had reduced to a pink glow and Kathryn felt really well.

Rafael thought the same that evening. "Ready to come into the world again?" he grinned.

"Just about!" She took a good look at him. "Where are you going, Beau Brummel?"

The pale grey suit fitted him admirably. From neatly brushed hair to well-polished shoes he was the successful business executive. "Got a gala event at the hotel tonight so I have to make an effort." He shot back a cuff to check the time. "How would you and Deborah like to visit Granada?"

"Granada?" Kathryn wasn't sure. "It's some way from here, isn't it?"

"Not too far," he answered. "I've got three days off so we could go on Wednesday morning and come back on Friday afternoon. A friend has invited us to stay at his house."

Three days of being together! The depth of her longing to go made Kathryn hesitate. She knew Rafael was asking out of kindness and she was appreciative but she realised her feelings for him could go a lot further if she wasn't careful. There was no point in creating problems for herself. "Thank you for the invitation but I don't want to go."

"Why not?"

He would ask the one question she wasn't prepared to answer. "I prefer not to."

"Think about it some more," he urged, glancing at his watch again. "Overnight you may change your mind. Granada is a beautiful city and you'll regret missing it. I'll ring you in the morning for your final decision."

Kathryn's 'That was my final decision,' got lost in his departure. Muttered comments on managers who think they can manage everyone punctuated Kathryn's evening. She was not going and that was that!

She was ready for the morning phone call, her lines rehearsed. Kathryn was taken completely off-guard by a woman's voice inquiring if she was Señora Morris.

"I am Francisca Sanchez," she introduced down the line. "I live in Granada with my family. We asked you up to stay with us only you felt unable to accept. I thought I would extend a personal invitation. Caspar and I would be delighted to welcome you to our home."

"It's very generous of you." Kathryn

was not quite sure how to deal with her unexpected caller.

"Not at all," she was assured. "We have two children so your little girl would have company. If there is a problem please say."

"Not a problem exactly!" Kathryn's arguments were of no use against the charming voice and she couldn't think of a good excuse.

"You have not known Rafael long and do not want to rush things," Francisca Sanchez guessed with such stunning accuracy Kathryn gasped. "Do not worry. We are not match-making busybodies who will embarrass you at every turn."

"It isn't like that," Kathryn disclaimed, recovering her balance. "Rafael and I are not . . . I mean . . . "

"You are two people who enjoy each other's company," Francisca said, "and no more."

"Right!" Kathryn agreed, grateful for the woman's understanding.

"Then come and enjoy it in Granada!

The city is truly lovely and you're sure to like it."

Rafael came down during the heat of the afternoon. He accepted her turn-about with a casual, "I knew you would once you'd thought it over."

He went off whistling to the outside storeroom oblivious to the dark look Kathryn gave him. He returned with two small cases, one of which he dropped on the floor by the bedroom door. "You won't need your large one for a couple of nights." He threw the other on the back seat of his car and drove away with a cheerful wave.

Rafael was in the same good humour early Wednesday morning, adding their case to his own in the boot.

"What are your friends like?" Kathryn asked after a few miles.

"Caspar and I were at school together," he replied. "Later we chose the same university where we met Francisca. She was my girl-friend for a while until I made the mistake of introducing her to Caspar. I soon became an also-ran."

Who very quickly found consolation in Olivia, Kathryn thought. "Did you mind?"

"There was nothing between Francisca and I. The three of us couldn't have remained friends if there had."

The journey gave Kathryn a chance to see a little of the Andalusian countryside.

"This is the province which always seems the most Spanish to an outsider," Rafael told her, "possibly because it's the most Moorish. Granada was held by the Moors for over seven centuries."

The Sanchez house was larger than Kathryn expected, its windows covered against the growing heat. Rafael blew the horn before getting their cases from the boot.

Francisca Sanchez was a calm woman of around thirty with brown hair and beautiful dark eyes. She greeted Kathryn warmly. "I am pleased to see you, and this must be Deborah."

Meanwhile her two children fell on

Rafael like a favourite uncle, both talking at once and pulling at him to get his attention.

"We'll leave them to it," Francisca told Kathryn. "Rafael knows his way about. Give me your case."

She led them into the house and up the stairs to a bedroom with a small balcony. The room was large with a tiled floor scattered with rugs. Heavy wardrobes which would have overpowered a smaller room stood along one wall matching the carved headboard of the double bed. A modern divan bed stood in the corner.

"I thought your daughter would like to be in with you." Francisca opened a door at the side to reveal a tiled bathroom. "Come down when you're ready."

On their own Kathryn and Deborah looked at one another in disbelief. Rafael's modest house on the coast had not prepared them for the size of this one, nor for the ornate tiling and wrought ironwork. After a wash they walked along a passage hung with pictures to the staircase. It descended with shallow treads to a wide hall decorated with a display of pot plants.

"We are outside." Francisca appeared in a doorway. "Come through."

The patio was bounded by the house on three sides and an eight-foot wall, broken by a gateway, on the other. The paved area had tubs of flowers spread about and a small fountain in the middle. Cushioned chairs together with a long table were set out in the deep shade against part of the house.

"Rafael is with the children," Francisca explained, pulling forward a chair for Kathryn. "We haven't seen him since Christmas and there's some catching up to be done."

Deborah went to examine the fountain, trailing her fingers in the cascading water.

"My husband usually comes home to lunch with us," Francisca went on, "but today he will work through so he can finish early. He has also arranged to have tomorrow off."

"You have a beautiful home," Kathryn remarked. "Have you lived here long?"

"Since we were married," Francisca replied. "Caspar's great-grandfather bought it and the family have been here from then. My parents-in-law occupy one part of it although they are away at the moment."

Running feet and laughter sounded within the house and Rafael arrived accompanied by the Sanchez children, a girl of eight with her mother's eyes and a boy of five just shedding the chubbiness of toddlerhood. Rafael took them over to meet Deborah, acting as an interpreter until the initial shyness wore off.

"The children adore him," Francisca commented. "We stay at his house in the spring and autumn to give the children some days by the sea." She watched Rafael with affection. "Not that we saw him this year, he was too busy!"

She turned her head to study

Kathryn. "That's really why I rang you. I thought he might not come if you didn't and he needs a break. Being close to the hotel like he is, he's always on call."

When Kathryn remained silent Francisca said, "I hope you are not offended by my honesty."

"Certainly not," Kathryn refuted. "I'm happy it's worked out as you wanted."

Rafael came to join them leaving the children to devise their own ways of communication.

"Tonight we will go out and show you some of the sights," Francisca promised her guest.

Caspar Sanchez arrived home at seven, removing tie and jacket whilst crossing from the gate. Kathryn accepted his translated comment on her fairness as the usual greeting. Caspar only spoke a word or two of English and Kathryn would dearly have liked to know what he said to produce the complacent look on Rafael's face. Francisca was in the house so she couldn't help.

After a light meal they all crammed in the family car and headed towards the city centre. Parking the car they ambled through the crowded streets, pausing now and then for a closer look. Two hours later, Kathryn requested a rest for Deborah. In a small café they all had a cooling drink.

"Tomorrow we'll visit the Alhambra," Rafael told Kathryn.

He and Caspar took the three children to look over a toy shop while Kathryn stayed with Francisca.

She ordered another drink for them. "Rafael tells me you are a swimming instructor. How do you deal with lots of children at once? I'd be hopeless."

Kathryn laughed. "It isn't that bad!"

"Rafael was full of praise over your rescue of Olivia's boy. That must have been difficult."

"Not too much!" Kathryn disclaimed.

Francisca turned her glass round and round. "What do you think of Olivia?"

"She appears a very confident woman, sure of herself and of what she wants." Kathryn aimed for impartiality.

Francisca's face set in hard lines. "She can also be very selfish. I don't know how Rafael can continue to work with her after what happened!" She broke off and gave Kathryn an embarrassed look. "I have said too much. Rafael would not like my gossiping."

"He told me of the engagement," Kathryn said.

Francisca was relieved. "You already know! It must be awkward at the hotel no matter what Rafael says to the contrary."

"It can't be or he wouldn't have chosen to work there," Kathryn remarked, watching the evening crowd strolling by.

"He didn't choose exactly!" Francisca revealed. "It was an unfortunate combination of circumstances."

Kathryn stared at her. "In what way?" She saw the indecision on the other woman's face and retracted. "I'm sorry. I shouldn't be prying into Rafael's private affairs."

"Hardly private," Francisca said bitterly, "not when half of it was blazed across the newspapers. Rafael had known Olivia before he and I were at university together because their fathers had some business connection. Both families were wealthy." Francisca rested her chin on both hands. "The two of them got engaged some months before I married Caspar. We came back from honeymoon to find the scandal all over the front pages."

Kathryn was immersed in the story, trying to imagine Rafael as a student.

"Rafael's father's business had collapsed leaving a vast pile of debts. Señor Delvega had a massive stroke and survived only a few days then the whole sorry mess fell into Rafael's lap."

"What on earth did he do?" Kathryn felt for the young Rafael. What a disaster!

"He sold everything to pay off the

151

creditors," Francisca recalled. "The family house, the cars, everything. The land next to his grandmother's house on the coast he gave to Olivia's father in settlement which is why the hotel is where it is."

"And Olivia?" Kathryn just had to know.

"For Rafael her reaction was the worst part." Francisca's caustic tone showed her feelings. "She broke off the engagement!"

Kathryn was appalled. "But her father was a wealthy man! She couldn't have wanted for money."

"It was the loss of status she couldn't take," Francisca spelled out. "She didn't want to be married to a bankrupt's son!"

Kathryn sat in shocked silence, thoughts churning, equating what she'd been told with Olivia's present attitude towards Rafael.

Francisca completed the story. "To his credit Olivia's father was furious, the more so when she married Jorge

Santini without his knowledge. He gave Rafael a job, moving him to the Mediterraneo as deputy manager once it opened. During his last illness he promoted Rafael to manager."

"Olivia wants Rafael now." Kathryn stared into her empty glass.

"She never stopped wanting him!" Francisca said scornfully. "It's taken her a while to realise the quality of a man doesn't lie in what he owns!"

Kathryn caught sight of her daughter and waved. The children each had a book, Deborah's being an illustrated counting one of numbers up to ten in Spanish.

"Rafael is going to help me," she told her mother.

Over Deborah's head Kathryn smiled her thanks at him. It was an indication of his strength of character that he could have gone through so much yet had not been soured. Her respect for him increased enormously.

They sauntered back to the car. Francisca insisted on going in the back so Kathryn sat between the two men in the front. She felt tired, saying little as the car travelled away from the centre. The sudden swing of the vehicle to avoid a scooter sent her heavily against Rafael. His arm came round her to anchor Kathryn to his side. She experienced a feeling of utter contentment spiced with anticipation. Was there more in Rafael's attitude than friendship? He had gone to a lot of trouble over her and Deborah.

Kathryn frowned into the darkness. She'd be wise to keep a tight rein on her emotions for it would never do to fall in love with Rafael.

At the house Rafael walked Kathryn and Deborah to their bedroom door. 'Night, tadpole." He tweaked the little girl's hair.

"Good night." Deborah opened the door. "Thank you for my book."

She went inside and Kathryn looked up with a gentle glow in her blue eyes. "It's been a lovely day."

"More tomorrow." As he had once

before, he kissed her very quickly. "Good night, little one."

Lying in bed Kathryn could still feel the slight pressure of his mouth on hers. What was Rafael up to? The unwelcome thought that he might just be amusing himself caused Kathryn severe misgivings.

Whatever he was doing she was determined to remain cool and detached. That way she would return home with no regrets.

6

KATHRYN was getting used to meals in two languages. The planning of the day over breakfast was a noisy affair.

"We could go round the shops," Francisca suggested to Kathryn, "although everywhere will be very busy."

"I'm not keen on the shops," Kathryn said. "When will we be able to visit the Alhambra?"

There was some quick Spanish, shaking of heads, then agreement. "Deborah, you and I can go later today," Rafael replied. "The others have seen it several times."

"What do you want to do, Francisca?" Kathryn asked.

"If we all feel lazy we could go to the park. The children like it and only the locals use it so there won't be a crowd."

Kathryn got a nod from Deborah. "Suits us."

"It does not seem very exciting," Francisca commented a while later. She and Kathryn were under a tree watching the men and the children play an exceedingly loud game of football. "We should have gone out."

"Don't worry on my account," Kathryn reassured. "This is fine for me and Deborah is having a great time."

The energetic kicking of Marino's ball was producing some wild results with shouting in both languages. Both men were as enthusiastic as the children.

"They are nothing but a pair of boys." Francisca stretched out on her stomach. "They have known each other so long and have similar tastes. Olivia could never understand that. I don't like her although I tried for Rafael's sake. She always treated me as an inferior. My family are ordinary people. Olivia behaved as though I was — how

157

would you say — ?"

"One of the common herd!" Kathryn supplied. "Like me!"

"*Si*, a peasant," Francisca confirmed laughing.

Joining in Kathryn flopped down beside her. It was cool beneath the tree despite the fast-climbing temperature. Twenty minutes later a halt was called in the football and the gasping players headed for the tree.

"That's my exercise for the week," moaned Rafael, lying flat out. "I may not be the same again!"

"Poor, weak thing!" Kathryn teased. "Being stuck in an office is making you soft."

He lifted his head. "I'll race you to that bush over there!"

"Not me! I'm even more unfit."

"Not the way you swim," Rafael corrected with a smile. "You probably run marathons in your spare time!"

★ ★ ★

Deborah was rather quiet following her afternoon rest. She watched Kathryn apply a thin layer of make-up, darkening her lashes to bring out their length. The pale blue dress with its frilled collar and wide sleeves made her look more fragile than she was.

"Are you ready, love?" Kathryn picked up her hat and bag.

"Do we have to go?" Deborah burst out.

Kathryn turned in surprise, one hand on the door knob. "We don't *have* to! Don't you want to?"

"It will be hot and crowded," Deborah complained. "I'll get a headache like I did last night. Benita won't be going."

"She's been before," Kathryn pointed out. "We're only here until tomorrow so there's just one chance."

"It's just an old building," Deborah protested.

Kathryn knew it was useless to try to explain why the Alhambra was worth several visits. She hid her disappointment, recognising that to a seven-year-old it wasn't so interesting. Deborah bounced along the passage in high spirits, her mother more subdued.

"I can see you're raring to go." On the patio Rafael stood up at their approach, car keys in hand.

Deborah looked uncertainly at Kathryn who stepped into the breach. "Do you mind if we don't go?"

He glanced from one to the other. "Why not?"

It was Kathryn again who answered. "Deborah found it rather trying in the city yesterday and doesn't want to go."

Rafael's gaze rested thoughtfully on the little girl's face then he rounded on Francisca watching from one of the padded chairs. "You don't mind having Deborah here while we go, do you?"

Francisca shook her head. "Go and enjoy yourselves."

It seemed a reasonable solution to Kathryn but her daughter kicked moodily at a flower-pot. "I thought we could go to the park again."

"We won't be long," Kathryn told her.

"I don't want to be on my own," Deborah grumbled.

"That's enough!" Kathryn ordered in a much firmer tone. "You won't be on your own and Benita has plenty of toys to keep you occupied."

Deborah refused to be placated. "I don't feel well."

"Then you can go to bed!" Rafael said. "Stop messing about, Deborah. You either come with us or stay here but I'm taking your mother so hurry and decide."

It was the sternest voice he'd ever used with the child. If Deborah started to cry Kathryn knew she'd change her own mind.

"I'll stay." Deborah kissed her mother good-bye though Rafael got a very resentful look.

They drove most of the way in silence, a lot of the delight gone from the trip for Kathryn. Parking the car they walked up the road and through the gateway into the Alhambra grounds. The change from city streets to green woodland lifted Kathryn's mood and some of the anticipation returned.

Further along the road, where it widened for a space, Rafael steered her to one side. "We can go back if you prefer," he said abruptly.

"I want to see it all," Kathryn replied at once.

His face cleared slightly. "Deborah will be fine with Francisca."

Kathryn put a hand on his arm. "I'm not worried, it's just that there's only Deborah and me. I'm not an indulgent parent ready to give in to every whim but it upsets me when we're at odds with one another."

"I understand." Rafael covered her hand with his own. "Let's go. It takes a while to see this place."

The Alhambra was a bewitching confection of the massive and the delicate. The tranquillity of small rooms and the serenity of the Court of Myrtles, its pool of water reflecting the ornate designs, contrasting with the series of towers squatting on the outer rim of the vast complex.

"I must buy a book to remind me of all this," Kathryn exclaimed halfway round, gazing in awe at the incredible columns and ceiling in the Court of Lions. "On wet winter days I'll remember the splendour."

Almost in a daze she wandered with Rafael along the tree-lined road towards the last gateway.

"You need to visit often to even begin to absorb the artwork," Rafael observed, turning a corner. "We will get a good variety of books along here."

After much deliberation Kathryn chose one that was mainly pictures instead of text.

"I'll write underneath in English for you," Rafael offered. "Right now I could do with a drink."

Kathryn hesitated, her thoughts turning to Deborah. They'd been away for three hours already and she didn't want her daughter getting into a state.

"We'll ring Francisca," Rafael suggested when she voiced her doubts. "See what's happening."

"It's you who is missing all the fun," Francisca informed Kathryn. "Some of Benita's friends have come. One of them has been learning the flamenco. She's busy teaching the others how to do it. Deborah is having a wonderful time so there is no need to hurry back."

"Benita and Deborah can give us a show this evening," Rafael said on hearing the news.

In good humour they joined the sauntering people and window-shopped their way down the street. Rafael held Kathryn's hand again making her feel part of the many couples on all sides. He paused so they could study the display in a jeweller's window.

"Shall we get something for Deborah?" Rafael pointed to a section containing children's items. "A chain or a bracelet?"

To Kathryn the shop didn't appear an expensive one and she was happy to go in for a look round. The assistant brought out a tray of bracelets, each one with a small charm attached to it. Kathryn was deliberating between a seashell and a sailing boat when Rafael noticed a display of filigree rings.

"I don't think so," Kathryn demurred. "The rate Deborah's growing a ring would soon be too small for her."

Rafael took an adult-sized one from the tray. "What about you?" He reached for her hand and slid the ring on to her third finger. "Your wedding ring looks a bit lonely on its own."

In horror Kathryn stared at the two rings side by side, a shudder running through her. "No!" she exclaimed in agitation and tore the silver ring from her hand. It was slammed on the counter and Kathryn was running from the shop heedless of Rafael's startled cry.

She kept up a furious pace until a hand on her arm swung Kathryn round to face a baffled Rafael. "What's the . . . ?" With a muttered word in Spanish he removed her dark glasses. The brilliant blue eyes were spilling tears.

"I'm all right." Her voice wobbled in contradiction to the words and she hunted in her bag for a handkerchief.

Retaining a grip on her arm Rafael hurried Kathryn to the car, hustling her in and driving away stony faced. He left the city and climbed into the hills off the main road. Running the car into a grassy space he switched off and came round to her door. "Come on." He pulled her from the seat. The slope was fairly steep to a level patch some thirty yards above the parked vehicle. "We'll sit here a while."

The sun was low in the sky, its dying rays illuminating the city. On its hill the Alhambra glowed golden in the soft light whilst, in the background, the snow on the Sierra Nevada gleamed whitely against the sky.

They sat in silence, together yet apart. Rafael was a little in front of Kathryn and she couldn't see his face properly. He had his arms on his raised knees, gaze on the distant mountains. Gradually Kathryn's whipped up emotions quietened in tune with the surroundings. Lights appeared across the city as the sun began to set — and still the two of them remained unmoving.

At last Kathryn put a hand on Rafael's shoulder and said, "I'm sorry for over-reacting."

He turned his head to look at her, puzzlement evident in his expression. "I greatly offended you. I apologise most sincerely."

"Your action did not offend me." She looked away from the keen gaze. "It reminded me of something I have done. It hurt me deeply and sometimes the pain comes back."

"Can I help?" His voice was full of concern.

Despondently Kathryn shook her head. "It's done now. I just haven't quite come to terms with it."

"It could help to talk about it," Rafael counselled. "No use bottling it up."

Kathryn linked her fingers together, the knuckles showing white. "I sold Colin's ring," she blurted out. "I promised Deborah we would come to Spain. She had been so ill I couldn't deny her. Then I became frantic because I couldn't afford it."

Consideringly Rafael said, "I thought the doctor had recommended some time in the sun for Deborah."

"He did!" Kathryn confirmed, "and Deborah wanted Spain." She drew a long breath. "I sold my engagement ring because I didn't want to get into debt. I don't know what Colin would have thought of it."

After a ruminative pause Rafael remarked in a very casual manner, "Hard unforgiving people are always difficult to deal with, even if . . . "

168

Kathryn was on her feet in a flash. "How dare you!" she erupted. "Colin was the kindest, most generous man I've met. He would have given his last penny to help."

Rafael came to his feet, a warm look in his dark eyes. "Which is what he did!" He put a hand on her shoulder and regarded her furious face. "He gave you the ring. Your husband paid for Deborah's holiday which is what you would expect from the man you described."

In the grip of rage, his words took a full minute to sink in then in a choked voice Kathryn said, "I hadn't thought of it like that!"

Rafael put his arms round her, holding Kathryn in a comforting embrace until she had recovered her composure.

"You made me mad on purpose," she accused, leaning back against his encircling arms.

"It stopped you feeling guilty and let you see the truth," he answered. "I refuse to apologise."

"Thank you," Kathryn said with grateful sincerity.

His embrace tightened and she waited for him to kiss her. Instead his arms fell away and he said, "I can barely see the car."

He took her hand to help Kathryn down the incline, both running the last few yards to the road.

★ ★ ★

"Guess what we've been doing!" Deborah burst out the moment she saw her mother.

"I can't think!" Kathryn simulated surprise.

After supper Francisca put on a record for Benita and Deborah to show how much they had learned.

"Come on, Mum." Kathryn was dragged from her chair.

Soon everyone was having a try, collapsing in shared laughter at the end. Rafael was the only one not too much out of breath.

"Today's been great," Deborah pronounced later, scrambling into bed. "I've really enjoyed myself."

"And me." Kathryn covered her daughter with the sheet.

Rafael was alone on the patio, turning round at the sound of Kathryn's step.

"I feel quite tired myself now," she yawned, sinking into a seat.

Francisca arrived carrying a tray of glasses and a bottle of wine. "A few quiet moments are called for before bed." She handed the bottle to Rafael to open as Caspar arrived from seeing their children to bed.

Kathryn knew this was one of the times she'd remember most. The secluded patio, filled with the scent of flowers, had an ageless charm. In the starry darkness the little fountain sang its endless song and all the world seemed at peace. She could readily understand Caspar and Francisca preferring to live in the family home instead of a modern apartment block.

Catching his wife yawning behind

her hand Caspar stood up. He wished Kathryn and Rafael good night, urged Francisca to her feet and escorted her inside.

Rafael divided the last of the wine into their empty glasses. "To you," he saluted, raising his. "May this be the first of many trips to Spain."

Kathryn picked up her own glass. "To you," she counter-proposed. "May your dreams become reality."

The look on his face made Kathryn gulp at her wine and remind herself this was the only visit she'd make to Spain. Holding her glass she wandered over to the fountain, away from the light, and let some of the water splash on to her fingers.

Rafael came to stand beside her. He took the glass and placed it on the fountain's rim. Turning Kathryn to face him he kissed her. Not a kiss-and-run affair like before but long and satisfying. Kathryn was powerless to stop the gradual build-up of emotion, feeling fulfilled yet oddly sad. She responded readily, savouring his closeness and latent strength.

Lifting his head Rafael slowly rubbed the side of his face against her hair. "You are very restful."

"So you've said before." Kathryn leaned her forehead on his shoulder aware she had to end this folly.

"Each time we meet you refresh me anew. You are a pool of clear water ready to revive and sustain."

"In other words a thorough drip!" Kathryn said in an attempt to break the mood. She forced a laugh. She went to step away only his hold stayed firm.

"What are you afraid of, Kathryn?"

The question stopped her short. "Nothing!" she denied without as much conviction as she wanted.

"Why are you running off like a startled deer?"

"What are you trying to make me say?" she demanded.

Close though they were the darkness obscured their faces, keeping expressions a secret.

"I have no intention of hurting you," Rafael said, sounding for once uncertain of his way.

"Hurting has nothing to do with intentions." Kathryn let the words hang between them before going on, "We have known each other barely four weeks. Like Luis I'd prefer not to drift out of my depth."

He murmured, "I understand," although Kathryn wasn't sure he did. Sleep was a long time coming. She lay in the darkness listening to her daughter's steady breathing across the room, every nerve tingling. It was years since she'd been so alive — or this unhappy!

All the self-warning had been useless. What she felt for Rafael was a deeper more mature love than she'd had for Colin, her teenage husband. That had been wiped out before it had had a chance to ripen.

And this one would fare no better, she despairingly acknowledged. It had happened quickly but Kathryn knew it would not die the same way. Part of her distress a few hours ago had been the shattering recognition over Rafael's casual gesture. She'd have given the world to have him put a ring on her finger — and mean it as Colin had done.

* * *

Pushing open the door of Rafael's house felt very like coming home. Kathryn looked around with a new awareness and stifled the longing for permanent residence. The journey had been uneventful following a noisy send-off by the Sanchez family in the early evening.

At the last moment Francisca gave Deborah a pair of castanets and a record. "Keep practising the flamenco," she told the delighted child. Turning to Kathryn she hugged her. "We have very much enjoyed having you here."

"Can you give me Francisca's address?" she asked Rafael after he'd carried the case into the bedroom. "I'd like to send a letter of thanks."

He wrote it on the kitchen pad before making some coffee. Kathryn came in from seeing Deborah into bed. "I enjoyed seeing Granada. I appreciate your taking us."

"I knew you'd like Caspar and his family which is why I invited you." He poured the coffee and they went to sit on the terrace. "It was a welcome break."

Kathryn kept the conversation light for another twenty minutes wishing Rafael would go, hoping he'd stay, calling herself every kind of weak-willed idiot. She closed the door behind him relieved he hadn't kissed her, and vaguely put out he hadn't even tried!

During the quiet of the next afternoon Kathryn wrote to Francisca thanking her for her warm hospitality. "We'll go to town to post it in the morning," she told Deborah.

To the child it was a game to search for the place selling stamps and then to watch Kathryn getting herself understood. The letter safely posted, they ambled along the sea front. Waiting to cross the road to catch the bus a car hooted at them. Olivia waved, "Do you want a lift?"

She was as coolly immaculate as ever in a white dress piped in navy and high-heeled sandals. "How did you like Granada?" She pulled smoothly away from the kerb.

"It has a unique atmosphere," Kathryn answered.

"I love it," Olivia confessed, "but Señor Sanchez and his wife are not my idea of fun."

"I found them lively," Kathryn said in surprise.

"I meant Caspar's parents," Olivia enlightened. "They are old-fashioned and do not approve of me." She flicked a glance at Kathryn. "Usually Caspar comes here to see us though occasionally, like now, Rafael feels duty-bound to go to Granada."

"He didn't act as if he considered

it a duty," Kathryn reviewed the three days. "In any case Caspar's parents weren't there."

The car wobbled slightly. "Did Rafael know they would be away?" Olivia's voice was sharp.

"I've no idea. You'll have to ask him."

Judging by her expression Olivia was not pleased by what she'd been told.

★ ★ ★

It was three long days before Rafael came again. Kathryn's guarded smile of welcome gave way to concern when she saw his face. "What have you been doing?" she demanded in consternation. "You look terrible!"

With red-rimmed eyes and haggard face he regarded her with weary appeal. "Mind if I stop for a while?"

"Of course not." Kathryn's reply was instant. "We were just going to have supper. Would you like some?"

Rafael rubbed his fingertips up and

down his forehead. "Not for me, thanks." He opened the fridge and pulled out a bottle of wine.

After Deborah was in bed Kathryn sat opposite Rafael and studied him. The wine bottle was two-thirds empty, his glass held loosely in clasped hands.

"Want to share your problems?" she gently probed.

The words started pouring out, an accent appearing for the first time. Kathryn listened, not saying anything. What he was detailing in steadily more graphic form was the daily stuff of his job and unlikely to knock him off balance so badly. When he eventually dried up she was no nearer a genuine reason.

"What time were you up this morning?" she asked, seeking a clue to his worn-out appearance.

"Unlike some people I never went to bed!" The harsh, bitter tone jolted Kathryn.

Rafael slumped in his chair, poured another glass of wine and tossed it off in a single go. He saw her expression. "I know! I shouldn't be drinking so much. I'll take myself off and stop disturbing you."

The wine hit him as he rose. Kathryn caught hold of him to stop the stagger.

"I'm all right!" He steadied and gazed down at her. "I'm not drunk, just one too many on an empty stomach." The car keys were produced from his trouser pocket. "Good night, Kathryn."

"You can't possibly drive." She whipped the keys out of his hand. "Leave the car until tomorrow."

"I'm not incapable!"

Kathryn put the keys behind her back and pleaded, "Please don't use the car."

She thought he'd take the keys then he suddenly shivered as though intensely cold. His fingers touched the side of her face. "You're right, Kathryn. Forgive me for being a nuisance."

There was no faltering in Rafael's stride up the drive. Kathryn bolted the door and leaned against it baffled by his visit. Knowing he was hurting, she'd felt frustrated by her inability to help. Sleep was too far away for her to go to bed so she sat in the chair until the sky began to pale before the dawn.

* * *

"Mum!" Deborah bounced into the bedroom the next morning. "Luis' mother is here. She wants to see you."

Olivia was fidgeting in one of the chairs, coming to her feet when she saw Kathryn. She looked a little less a fashion plate than usual and her face carried colour high on the cheekbones.

"Sorry to keep you waiting," Kathryn apologised. "I overslept."

With a rasp Olivia said, "That is understandable!"

Something had put the woman in a raging temper and Kathryn felt unequal to dealing with her. "You don't mind if I have my breakfast, do you!" She

181

went into the kitchen. Only Olivia's car stood on the drive.

Kathryn took her breakfast on to the terrace. "Would you like a coffee?"

"No!" Olivia snapped. "I would like to know what happened here last night."

Kathryn was at a loss. "Last night?"

"I caught some of the hotel waiters having a good laugh. One of them came past here on his way to work and saw Rafael's car parked in the drive."

Kathryn reached for a piece of bread. "So what?"

"So what!" Olivia slammed her bag on the table making everything rattle. "Small wonder you overslept. It must have been a very active night!"

Kathryn paused in her buttering. "You have a very suspicious mind. The car was here, Rafael was not. He had some wine and decided not to drive after it."

"You surely do not expect me to believe that!"

Olivia's derisive tone needled Kathryn.

182

"It is a matter of indifference to me what you believe. I don't have to excuse or explain my conduct to you." The blue gaze was very bright. "I should be surprised to learn Rafael does either."

For a space they stared at one another then Olivia swung round, walked to the wall and looked down at the beach. Kathryn continued with her breakfast keeping a wary eye on the other woman.

Olivia came back to the table and sat down. "I will have a coffee. I am under such a strain at the moment I scarcely know what I am doing. Hearing the waiters gossiping about me was not pleasant."

"About you!" Kathryn was amused by all the fuss. "I thought I was the object of their ribaldry."

Olivia drooped. "They know how things are between Rafael and me. Spaniards find other people's private business vastly interesting."

All desire to be amused fled from

183

Kathryn. "And what are things between you and Rafael?"

The blunt question caused Olivia's eyes to widen. She cast a quick glance round as though in search of eavesdroppers. "We will marry soon."

"It's been decided!" Even to her own ears Kathryn's voice sounded tight.

Olivia smiled in quiet triumph. "It was decided many years ago. At the moment Rafael is busy playing games and making me wait. Maybe even punishing me for what I did but we understand each other, he and I. The same Andalusian heat blazes in our veins. In the end we will be as one. He knows this as well as I."

Supreme self-confidence wrapped round her like a cloak and it was Kathryn who felt like drooping now. "I offer my congratulations to you both."

Olivia laughed. "Please do not say that to Rafael or he will make me wait an extra six months."

In curiosity Kathryn asked, "What would you have done if Rafael had stayed here last night?"

"Nothing!" Olivia's expression was very worldly wise. "You are of the frigid north and do not understand these things. Rafael and I are children of the sun, sometimes distracted by passing fancies. Neither of us place much value on such diversions."

Olivia was right! Kathryn did not understand! The relationship explained across the breakfast table was totally beyond her comprehension.

Collecting her bag Olivia stood. "By the way, how was Rafael last night?"

Kathryn was a little guarded. "How do you mean?"

"He has been rather moody for a day or two. I wondered how he was with you."

As clear as the sky above her head Kathryn knew Olivia was the cause of Rafael's disturbed state. This tearing at the person you were supposed to love was something else Kathryn couldn't comprehend. "He was the same as usual," she lied.

Her unwelcome visitor saw the time and clicked her tongue. "I must be going. I have to travel to Madrid today. My ex-husband is flying over to see Luis and I want to be there."

"He doesn't live in Spain?"

"For the past year he has lived in America."

★ ★ ★

By dint of hard mental discipline and physical exertion Kathryn was able to push the visit from her mind and enjoy the day with Deborah. Rafael's car arriving halfway through the next afternoon set her nerves jangling. Was he missing his 'lady love' away in Madrid? Recalling the way he had dismissed his involvement with Olivia as something in the past Kathryn could only marvel at her own gullibility. Her cool welcome was covered by Deborah's enthusiastic one.

"I have a surprise for you," he greeted the child, crouching down so their faces were level. "What would you most like to watch?"

Deborah pondered, her face screwed up in deep thought then her eyes rounded in a hardly-daring-to-hope expression. "Dancing!" she breathed.

"Dancing it is!" Rafael straightened, his face sobering as he looked at Kathryn. "There's a flamenco troupe in town for two nights. We can go this evening."

Kathryn was given no chance to answer. "What time?" Deborah demanded.

The arrangements were made then in a low tone he said, "Thank you for the other night."

"I didn't do anything." Kathryn was off-hand.

"You listened," he said. "It was a great help."

The frigid folk from the north are good for something, she gloomily reflected.

"I'd like to explain to you," Rafael was saying. "Perhaps tonight when

Deborah is in bed."

"You don't owe me an explanation," Kathryn refuted in immediate haste. Having Rafael describe the twists and turns of his private life would be too much to bear.

He gave her a searching look. "I want you to understand."

I understand only too well! You're just amusing yourself until matters are settled with Olivia. I'm conveniently placed to be used!

Deborah could hardly contain her excitement over the proposed visit and Kathryn took the bubbling child to the beach to keep her occupied. They inadvertently stayed too long, scrambling up the steps and dashing between bedroom and bathroom to be ready on time.

Stationed at the kitchen window Deborah watched for the first glimpse of Rafael's car. An hour passed very slowly. When the phone rang they both jumped.

"Señora Morris? I have a message

from Señor Delvega." The unfamiliar voice carried a heavy accent. "He has been called away unexpectedly. He tried to contact you. Please accept his apologies."

"Thank you for ringing," Kathryn said automatically.

"It was a pleasure. I expect Señor Delvega will make his apologies in person when he returns from Madrid."

Half-numbed Kathryn stuttered, "He's gone to Madrid?"

"*Si*, Señora Morris. There was a call from Señora Santini and he left at once."

Deborah cried herself to sleep. It was only sheer willpower that stopped Kathryn from doing the same.

7

"WE'll have to go to town in the morning," Kathryn told Deborah on Monday evening. "I want to check how we get to the airport on Friday."

At the Hotel Christoval the courier was as helpful as ever, checking their ticket and arranging a taxi. "You don't fancy a coach trip, do you? I could do with a couple more. It's a tour of the local area and you see places normally awkward to reach."

"What's the return time?" Kathryn wanted to get a present for the neighbour looking after their flat.

"The shops will still be open," the courier confirmed, "and lunch is included in the price."

Thinking the opportunity to see a little more of the country was too good to miss Kathryn booked two seats.

It left her enough for a moderate shopping trip. Quarter of an hour later the coach climbed out of the town. For a while they travelled the coast road, the sea lapping rocks and beaches, its surface sparkling under the cloudless sky, then the coach turned inland.

Lunch was taken at a leisurely pace in an outdoor restaurant. Kathryn found the company of other English holiday-makers refreshing, especially as everyone was in a good mood.

They reached town half an hour before the shops shut and managed to find a suitable present for their neighbour. A slow stroll brought the two of them to catch the local bus on the outskirts. Kathryn had managed to keep Rafael at the back of her mind for the day — which was the right place for him. In a few days they would be home and this summer madness would fade in the icy winds of an English winter. If part of her refused to believe that Kathryn chose to ignore it.

Deborah hopped and skipped down the drive. "I don't want any supper," she announced. "My tummy's still full of lunch."

"It certainly was a big one," Kathryn agreed, searching her bag for the key.

She was about to insert it when the door was wrenched open from the inside. Kathryn let out a cry of surprise, jumping back a step.

Face like an overcast day Rafael glowered at the two of them. "Where have you been? You've been gone for hours."

Recovering Kathryn ushered Deborah inside. "On a day trip," she coldly informed him. "The next time give me some warning of your presence."

"I didn't mean to startle you." The stiff apology did little to mollify Kathryn.

She was as curt as him. "What do you want?"

"To explain about Saturday evening." He looked down at Deborah. "I'm so sorry about the dancers."

"Are they still here?" she asked hopefully.

"They were only here for two nights." He sounded genuinely regretful. "Where have you been today?"

Rafael sat on the arm of a chair to listen. He certainly had a way of charming Deborah and making her forget the hurt of Saturday. Kathryn sat across the room contributing little to the conversation.

Now that Rafael had recovered his good humour she could see the change in him. He was fairly bubbling with animation, a far cry from the disheartened man of Thursday. Whatever had happened in Madrid unquestionably agreed with him! An idea of what it must be depressed Kathryn. The thought that Rafael and Olivia really did deserve one another was only briefly comforting. They were together, she was alone.

"I am truly sorry about Saturday," Rafael apologised again after Kathryn had put Deborah to bed. "Was she very upset?"

"It was all over the next day." She remained standing ready to see him off.

"I would like to explain," Rafael began.

"You don't have to," Kathryn hastily broke in. "I know you're busy with many calls on your time."

"It was important or I wouldn't have let you down."

"A change of plan can happen to any one." She looked pointedly at her watch.

Some of the eagerness disappeared from Rafael's expression. "Is anything the matter? You seem on edge."

"No," Kathryn denied. "I'm rather tired."

"You would prefer not to talk now?" She could see he was puzzled by her attitude.

"Some other time," Kathryn suggested. With luck she'd be able to avoid him for the last few days of the holiday.

"If you insist." His restrained tone spoke volumes. "I'll call you tomorrow."

When the phone rang after breakfast Kathryn had a craven impulse to leave it unanswered.

"Good morning, Señora Morris." Olivia Santini's smooth voice came down the line. "Would you like to lunch with me today? I know you are going home in a day or two so there won't be another opportunity. Bring your little girl and I will make arrangements for her."

Kathryn accepted without much enthusiasm. At least she'd be out of the house if Rafael called. At the hotel he could hardly buttonhole her under his employer's watchful eyes — assuming that's what Olivia still was!

Nothing in Kathryn's wardrobe could compete with Olivia's elegance so she wasted no time in trying, selecting the blue dress with the faint self-stripe.

"Will Luis be there?" Deborah asked on the way.

"His mother never said."

Olivia came down in response to the receptionist's call. She smiled at Deborah. "I have found someone for you to play with. It is boring listening to adults talking."

Her high heels clicked on the tiled floor as she led the way from the foyer to the rear garden. The plain black dress she was wearing showed off her good figure but drained the colour from her face. Contrary to her usual habit she wore no jewellery except a small ring. Generally she appeared more subdued and lacking vitality.

Olivia took them over to a young woman in charge of two children. They were English, the little girl welcoming someone to play with as her brother was only three.

"I'll see Deborah has lunch," the woman assured Kathryn. "My job will be easier with Liza occupied."

Thanking her, Kathryn walked through the grounds with Olivia. Going inside the hotel owner rang for the lift. "We will have lunch now. I have ordered it in my suite."

The view from the balcony overlooking the swimming-pool was quite spectacular. Rafael's house could just be discerned through the belt of trees, its beach hidden by the rocky headland. Like a glittering invitation the sea gleamed and sparkled under the arching sun, undulating to timeless rhythms, constant and unending. Kathryn felt its lure even as she recognised its menace. She could see one or two swimmers braving the fierce heat, diving from the rocks which formed the hotel boundary.

They ate at a table set near the open balcony doors, Olivia serving from a trolley brought by a shirt-sleeved waiter. A bottle of wine chilled in an ice bucket. Kathryn smiled inwardly. How the other half lives!

"Tell me about your life in England." Olivia handed Kathryn a plate. "Where do you come from?"

To keep some kind of conversation going Kathryn described the new flat before moving on to the general locality. She wouldn't have expected Olivia to be particularly interested in her life yet the other woman listened with close attention, putting in the occasional comment and question.

"I envy you," she said at the end.

Kathryn paused, fork on the way to her mouth. "You envy me!"

Olivia gave a sad smile. "You have so much."

Kathryn flashed a quick glance around the spacious room with its matching furniture, cool tiled floor and neatly arranged paintings on the wall facing the sea.

"It is only a place to live in," Olivia said, watching the direction of her eyes.

"Only!" The single word contained a lot of feeling. "My entire flat would fit into this room!"

"You have other things." Olivia was gazing despondently into her wine.

Bluntly Kathryn stated, "You have it all."

Olivia shook her head. "Once I thought so, now it is different."

"Nonsense!" Kathryn strove for a bracing note. "You've had an upsetting time recently with the divorce and moving from Madrid." She put her napkin on the table ready to leave. "All that is behind you and the future is bright. You told me so yourself."

"The last time I spoke to you I believed it was." Dark eyes, bright with tears, were raised to Kathryn's face. "In Madrid my world fell apart."

"Trouble with your ex-husband?"

"That I expected!" Olivia seemed almost too choked to speak. "It was Rafael!" Her voice broke. "How could he have treated me so!"

Kathryn stiffened, an uneasiness of things better left unsaid spreading through her. "Rafael?"

Olivia left the table and roamed about the room, clasping and unclasping her hands, finally stopping by a large flower arrangement set on a chest beneath a wide mirror. She pulled at one of the blooms. "I have always known how much I hurt him. I was young and very silly. Instead of standing by him I ran away and have regretted it every day since." Flower petals began to drift to the floor. "My marriage was a disaster and I came home to my father's house bringing Luis with me. He was just a baby then."

She left the mutilation of the flowers and returned to the table. "We lived quietly until my father died. I met Rafael again at the funeral. He still felt the same. It was there in his eyes, in his every glance, every touch."

"Why didn't you marry then?" Kathryn was pleased her voice was steady.

"I was already married." Olivia sipped the remains of her wine, grimacing over its warmth. "At long last Jorge wrote to say he wanted a divorce. Everything was settled and I waited for Rafael to speak."

"And did he?" there was the slightest huskiness this time.

"Not in so many words!" The glass was banged down. "He resented any interest in other men but kept me waiting himself. Then Jorge arrived from America to see Luis. When I met him in Madrid I was horrified to learn Jorge intended taking our boy back with him. I begged and pleaded with no success." Her eyes went very hard. "I rang Rafael to come to help. He came all right! But not to help! He agreed with Jorge!"

Her fury grew while Kathryn watched in apprehension. "I have lost my son and Rafael is pleased! All this time he has been waiting for his revenge. Now he has it. I am alone and betrayed!"

Feeling she was being swept along on a tide of high drama Kathryn attempted to cut through the histrionics to the truth. "What did Rafael say in Madrid?"

Olivia pushed back her chair. "That he never intended marriage! It was a misunderstanding on my part."

"Could it have been?" Kathryn's

astringent tone made Olivia jerk up.

Voice full of angry sarcasm she said, "When a man says he wants to share his life with you and can't face the future without you, what is there to misunderstand! When he accompanies it with a ring . . . " Olivia thrust out her hand for Kathryn's inspection, " . . . the fact that he does not actually say 'marry me' goes unnoticed!"

Kathryn stared at the finely wrought gold ring set with tiny red stones. Somewhere inside a pain was gnawing, one that would get a lot worse. Rafael, she silently wept, what happened to you?

"Why do I wear it!" Olivia tugged the ring from her finger and tossed it into the ice bucket then regarded Kathryn thoughtfully. "You have trouble in believing all this, do you not?"

"A little," Kathryn admitted. "It seems so unlike Rafael. He's so honest and open, not . . . "

"You know little of him!" Olivia interrupted with a short laugh. "I am

202

sure you still think of him as an employee here."

Kathryn stared. "He isn't!"

"That was our little joke," Olivia said. "True, Rafael managed the hotel. He is also part-owner. In case you never discovered what he was doing at the Christoval the day you arrived he owns that as well."

Stunned Kathryn whispered, "Why did he never say?"

Olivia got up. "You might have become a nuisance. Men are often pursued for their wealth. He offered you the use of his house as he couldn't help feeling sorry for you. He guessed you did not have much money."

Kathryn walked on to the balcony and surveyed the grounds. Someone was splashing in the pool and faint sounds came from beneath the umbrellas. She felt oddly detached from reality. "I wonder why he asked me to stay longer?" she mused out loud.

"Because of me!" Olivia came out beside her. "I was jealous of you in his house. I tried not to show it but he knows me too well. It is also the reason he took you to Granada."

Not for the world would Kathryn have admitted how hard she was trying to find flaws in Olivia's story and failing. Even allowing for exaggeration it had the ring of cold truth! Desperately she said, "Where did he get the money for the hotels?"

"He inherited it from his grandmother along with the house."

Kathryn gave up the futile attempt. She was strong enough to face the truth and live with it. Rafael was not the man she'd believed him to be although Kathryn would always be grateful for their time in Spain for Deborah's sake. Very composed she thanked Olivia for lunch. Going down in the lift she exerted a rigid control on her emotions.

She needed it when Rafael called her name in the foyer. She had assumed he wasn't here. Foolish considering he owned a slice of it!

"Looking for me?" He smiled and Kathryn felt the pull of his attraction for her.

"No, for Deborah." Her smile was non-existent. "She's playing with one of your young guests."

"I'll help you look."

"No need." Kathryn was coolly dismissive. "I can find her by myself."

"No trouble." He walked with her. "I'm about finished for the day."

So am I, thought Kathryn. She caught sight of Deborah waving from the other side of the pool. Kathryn waved back before holding out her hand to Rafael. "I'd like to say good-bye and thank you once again for your kindness over the house."

Rafael had taken her hand then frowned at her words. "You sound as though you were going this minute," he commented. "I'll be down to see you later today."

"I would rather you didn't."

He put his hands in his pockets. "You've been very evasive over the last few days. If you don't want me to come, just come straight out and say so."

"All right!" Kathryn was goaded into saying. "I don't want you to come."

"Why not?"

Kathryn glared at him. "I don't need a reason."

"For me you do!" The dark eyes had narrowed and she didn't care for the expression on his stern features.

To save further argument Kathryn started round the pool towards Deborah, annoyed that Rafael remained one step behind. The two girls were all smiles and Kathryn thanked the children's nurse who brushed them aside. "One more didn't matter. I hope you enjoyed your lunch."

Out of the corner of her eye Kathryn caught Rafael's reaction to the words. To avoid more questions she sat down in Deborah's seat and asked what the two of them had been doing. Rafael hovered restlessly for a few minutes then left with a parting 'I'll see you later' to Kathryn. Underneath her smiling talk with the woman she fretted and fumed over Rafael's inability to take no for an answer.

A little after eight the sound of a car on the drive brought Kathryn out of her chair, temper simmering. Marching across to the door she flung it back to come face-to-face with a smiling Jane Rodise.

"I've brought the new arrival to show you." She lifted the shawled bundle in her arms.

Kathryn's gaze dropped to the baby, all anger fleeing. "How nice to see you."

Behind Jane, her husband and Rafael were walking from the car.

"We've been to the Mediterraneo to see the people Tomas used to work with," Jane explained. "I insisted on coming to see you. We won't stay long."

"I'm glad you came." The emphasis was unconscious though Rafael didn't think so, his expression hardening into uncompromising lines. "Sit down and let me have a good look at the baby."

Jane subsided into a chair. "This little imp arrived the day after your last visit to us. We have named her Pilar for Tomas' grandmother."

"How do you feel?" Kathryn asked.

"Tired!" Jane replied. "It was rather a long labour. I'll spare you the grisly details."

Tomas groaned. "One small baby and the two of us are running round in circles." He nudged Rafael in the ribs. "You bachelors do not know how lucky you are!"

Rafael didn't look as though he thought he was lucky. His face was drawn, his body tense. Kathryn asked after old Señora Rodise and the talk became general. She described Granada which brought Rafael into the conversation.

"Can you stay for supper?" Kathryn looked from Jane to Tomas. "The kitchen is overflowing with food."

They exchanged nods and agreed.

The baby stirred and began to cry.

"I'll hold her for a while," Kathryn offered. "You must need a rest." She loved the touch of the tiny warm body against her, reviving memories of years ago. Pilar snuffled into sleep, her head under Kathryn's chin.

Jane smiled. "I can see you haven't lost the knack. Why haven't you got half-a-dozen?" She realised what she'd said and apologised. "How tactless of me."

"Colin and I planned to have at least two," Kathryn revealed, not offended by the casual remark. "Most days Deborah seems like two so I'm not missing anything."

Her daughter grinned at this aspersion and they all went on to the terrace to eat.

"Have a safe journey home," Jane said when it was time to go. "Please write to me."

Kathryn was acutely conscious of Rafael at her side as the car pulled away. The warmth of the night wrapped round them, a slight breeze ruffling through the bushes. In forty-eight hours she'd be looking at stars in an English sky and preparing, as best she could, to forget the man sharing this view with her. Her hands clenched in silent agony remembering her reaction in the jeweller's shop over the ring. Olivia, heaven help her, had Rafael's ring and look where it had got her!

Rafael was watching her closely. "Did you enjoy your lunch today?"

Kathryn walked inside. "The food was delicious. You have some excellent chefs."

"Was the company as good?" Rafael's question was rasped from behind her.

"To be truthful, no!" Kathryn turned to look at him. "Too much fire and passion for the lunch table."

Once he would have laughed. Now he was devoid of expression, just the glitter deep in his eyes that could have been due to anger. "What was she worked up about this time?"

"Everything!" Kathryn walked past

him with a pile of plates.

"And me in particular!" He leaned against the kitchen door regarding her heavy-browed.

"You're not Olivia's favourite person at the moment." Kathryn placed a half-empty dish in the fridge.

"I don't appear to be in favour with you either! You've been stand-offish since the last day in Granada."

He had no right to put such bitterness in his tone or comment adversely on her behaviour when his own was so deplorable. "Not stand-offish, merely cautious."

"Does being cautious include acting as though you can't bear to be in my company for more than five minutes at a time!" There was plenty of bite in his tone.

Kathryn achieved a light laugh. "You're exaggerating, Rafael."

"Am I?" He moved forward until he was right in front of her. "You're scared I might kiss you again. I remember the way you reacted when I did in Granada.

For a while you lit up like a torch."

Grasping the nettle Kathryn said, "I'm a normal woman. When I get kissed by an attractive man I respond." Her blue gaze met his unflinchingly. "That doesn't mean I want him to do it again or try to take matters further."

Very softly Rafael jeered, "Are you afraid you might learn something about yourself?"

Kathryn shook her head. "I know all there is to know about me. It's you I don't seem to know much about although Olivia filled in a few of the gaps."

"I might have guessed she'd spin some stories." The derisive note deepened. "And you believed them!"

Kathryn faced him, one hand on the door. "You mean you're not the owner of the Christoval? Not part-owner of the Mediterraneo?" His silence answered her. "Shall we agree Olivia was telling the truth!"

Kathryn went into the living-room to tell Deborah it was time for bed. "Are you and Rafael having a row?" she asked whilst undressing. "You sounded like it."

"No," Kathryn assured her. "A serious discussion." She kissed her daughter before turning off the bedroom light. As she closed the door Rafael came out of the other bedroom dressed in bathing trunks. "You're never going swimming in the dark!" she exclaimed.

"I often do it," he retorted, strode through the terrace doorway and down the steps.

After a struggle with herself Kathryn ran to the terrace wall. "Rafael! Come back. It isn't safe."

He gave no sign of hearing her, running round the turn in the steps and disappearing from view. In disgust Kathryn stamped into the house. She would *not* worry over a man who was being as troublesome as a small child. She'd go to bed and leave him to it!

Only it wasn't that simple. Irritation rising Kathryn went outside again to see if Rafael was returning. The breeze was freshening and she could hear the sea on the rocks. Twenty minutes and the annoyance had changed to unease. Thirty minutes and Kathryn could stand it no longer. She made a quick trip to the bedroom to check Deborah was asleep then hastened down the steps, slowing towards the bottom where the terrace lights didn't reach.

She stood and listened for a few minutes, the breeze tugging the hem of her dress. She moved forward until she was at the edge of the water. Straining her eyes, Kathryn tried to scan the dark surface from one rocky outcrop to the other. She walked along the water-line, a curious fluttering in the pit of her stomach.

"Rafael!" Raising her voice, she shouted even louder. "Rafael!"

"Looking for me!" he asked from behind her.

Kathryn whirled round with a scream of startled nerves. His sudden materialisation had her heart pounding.

"You fool!" she raged, shock and utter relief bringing her close to tears. "Walking up on me like that!" She couldn't stop shaking.

One step and his arms were round her, holding her quivering body against his own. "I'm sorry for frightening you."

Finding him safe made Kathryn madder than ever. "You're worse than a child!"

"I know." One hand stroked her short hair.

"You deserve to drown."

"I know that, too!"

"Stop agreeing with me," Kathryn stormed, pushing away from him. "A man your age should . . . " Realisation came. "You're not even wet!" She could still feel the warmth of his skin on her cheek.

"I decided not to swim." Rafael was smiling now, hands on hips. "I was over by the rocks thinking. I didn't see you until you were by the water."

Words failed Kathryn. While she'd

been imagining all kinds of disasters, he'd been calmly taking his ease on the sand. With a sound of frustrated anger she turned on her heel. The soft sand hampered her steps forcing Kathryn to slow her pace.

"I'm grateful for your concern." Rafael found it simple to keep up with her.

"Not concern," Kathryn huffily denied. "I can't sleep with the outside lights blazing."

"I thought you'd rushed down to perform another daring sea rescue."

She could hear the laughter in his voice and fumed all over again. Reaching the top Kathryn switched off the lights and locked the terrace door. Rafael had gone into the main bedroom and Kathryn slumped into a chair to await his return.

"Want some coffee?" He headed for the kitchen.

"No," she replied, following him, "and could you have yours at the hotel."

"Fair enough." Rafael was not in the least put out. In fact he seemed uncommonly cheerful. "I'll come down some time tomorrow and we'll arrange about the airport on Friday."

"I've booked a taxi," Kathryn frostily said.

Almost lazily he reached for her. "You're going independent on me again. I'll see to everything." His hold shifted, the warmth of his body pervading hers.

Kathryn twisted her head to avoid the kiss, totally furious, totally despairing that he could effortlessly arouse her emotions. "Let me go, Rafael," she said between gritted teeth. "I'm not in the mood for your Casanova act."

"It's no act," he whispered into her ear, his breath stirring the short strands of fair hair.

"No, it isn't!" Kathryn tore away. "It's part of you. Make up to a woman but don't put any feeling into it. Just a game to be played. I may be staying in this house but you're not using me."

She backed away.

His expression altered immediately, the good humour vanishing to be replaced by something Kathryn didn't like at all. "So you think I'm playing around!"

"It's quite obvious you are," she returned, "and I'm not interested."

"What a pity!" He came swiftly forward, the strange glitter once again deep in his eyes. Kathryn moved too late. "You're such a delightful playmate."

He had her pinned to the wall kissing her, not with the gentle passion of which he was capable but hard, punishing, seeking a truth Kathryn refused to give him.

"If you've quite finished," she threw at him in scathing tones, "you can go!"

His laugh was a shade uncertain. "Trying to evict me from my own house."

"Either you go or I will!" Kathryn faced up to him hiding her distress.

"I'm sure Olivia would find us accommodation."

He raked unsteady fingers through his black hair and turned to go. At the door he looked back. "Good night, Kathryn."

For an instant they stared at one another. There was nothing yet so much in the silence. Then he was gone, the crunch of his feet on the gravel drive fading into the night.

Kathryn secured the door feeling lost and forlorn. All her strength would be needed to fill the void opening inside her. She knew no amount of telling herself he wasn't worth the heartache would prevent one second of it.

She'd occasionally wondered how their last meeting would be. Kathryn had never thought it would encompass such bitter emptiness, resentment and cold pain.

8

"WE'LL have to go to town today, Mum," Deborah announced over the breakfast table. "I want to get Rafael a present."

Great! thought Kathryn. What do you give a man with two hotels — well, one and a half?

"I do like Rafael," Deborah confided for the umpteenth time on the way round the shops. "I want to get something special for him."

'Something special' took a lot of finding. Kathryn's patience began to wear thin even though, she admitted in disgust, she was as anxious as her daughter to give Rafael a memento of their visit. Deploring her ambiguity towards him Kathryn walked past a shop and was called back by Deborah. She was pointing to some small straw donkeys, wearing wide-brimmed hats, at the front of the window.

"Not those," Kathryn demurred. They were typical tourist items and she didn't consider them suitable. Turning to move on her attention was caught by a framed print on one side. She studied the label glad her memory hadn't failed her. It was the Alcazaba at Almeria. "Remember," she reminded Deborah. "Rafael took you round while I watched the boats."

When Rafael looked at it he would think of Deborah more than her mother. On that score he might not consign it to the dustbin.

Having already decided to leave the present at the Mediterraneo on their way home, Deborah had written a note thanking Rafael for the time at his house. "And thank you for the duck," she'd added. At the hotel Kathryn sent her daughter across to the reception while she waited by the main door. The receptionist came round to talk to Deborah, bending down to take the parcel and nodding.

"Rafael isn't here at the moment," Deborah informed her mother on her return.

"Probably visiting his other property," Kathryn muttered acidly, pushing open the door and emerging in to the sunlight.

"He'll come to see us later." Deborah skipped along at her side.

"Have you invited him?" Kathryn was not pleased.

"No but he'll come," the little girl said with confidence. "He'll want to say good-bye."

"Rafael is very busy so don't be surprised if he can't make it." Kathryn tried to prepare Deborah for the inevitable disappointment. At lunch she said, "We can spend the afternoon on the beach and pack tonight."

They had a good swim before lying on the loungers. Deborah soon fell asleep but her mother's mind was too active to do the same. No matter in which direction she sent them her thoughts kept returning to

Rafael. Making her believe he only worked at the luxury hotel! Her mind boggled at the probable value of the place. On top of which he had the Christoval, too.

As for Olivia! Kathryn imagined Rafael putting the ring on the woman's finger, telling her how much he wanted her, voice husky with emotion. Kathryn stirred restlessly, vainly trying to banish the images from her mind, jealousy flaring. Don't be a fool, she chided herself. He threw Olivia aside without a moment's hesitation and would do the same to you if he had any inkling of your true feelings. He was a man for the fun times, not one to ride out the storm with.

Around seven Kathryn decided reluctantly it was time to clear the beach after this final session. "We'll take the loungers up first."

Deborah wasn't listening, her gaze fixed beyond Kathryn. "Rafael," she shouted and was off, bounding up the beach like a whippet.

Rafael caught her flying figure and swung the child high in the air, making her laugh and shriek. Carrying her he came towards the shelter, moving easily over the warm sand. Kathryn stood stiffly by the folded lounger unable to think of anything to say.

"I told you, Mum!" Deborah chortled. To Rafael she said, "Mum didn't think you would come today."

After the most cursory of nods to Kathryn, Rafael gave his attention to Deborah. "I had to come to see my favourite blonde before she went home." He winked and the child giggled. "And to say thank you for my present. I'm going to choose a good place to hang it." He looked over to where the inflatable duck was lying by the water's edge. "Shall we give Daffy a last dip?"

Feeling left out Kathryn watched him strip off his jeans and chase Deborah into the water. She folded the other lounger and carried both of them up to the storeroom behind the house.

Picking up the holdall for the shelter she slowly returned to the beach. Ignoring the laughing antics in the water she dismantled the frame and carefully folded the covering. Once the shelter was stowed in the holdall Kathryn got her own belongings together.

Deborah ran from the water grabbing for a towel. Her face was flushed with exertion, eyes bright. "I could stay here forever," she panted.

"School starts next week," Kathryn reminded her.

Deborah rubbed her hair. "Who wants to go to school!"

"Carry the duck up to the house." Kathryn's rapped-out order gained her a surprised glance.

"Sure thing." Deborah set off at once, knowing her mother's tone from experience.

Kathryn and Rafael reached for the shelter holdall at the same moment, his hand closing over hers. She shot back, half tripping in her haste.

"For heaven's sake!" Rafael exploded.

"It was accidental. I have no intention of touching you."

"It wasn't like that yesterday," Kathryn retaliated, embarrassed by her own over-reaction.

"That was then!" Rafael picked up the holdall. "I have no wish to persist where I'm not welcome."

"We'd better go then," she snapped. "I'm sure you don't have time to waste, not with your hotel chain to run."

The holdall was dumped on the sand. "Listen to me, Kathryn," he ordered in exasperation. "I would have told you about the hotel business but . . . "

"Wealthy men have to be careful," Kathryn interrupted, all the injustice rising like a high tide. "Don't want to get tangled with fortune-hunters!"

The rage emanated from him like a tangible force swirling around her. "You are more of a child than Deborah! Too foolish for your own good and too naïve for the real world in which the rest of us live!"

"What would you know about the

real world!" Kathryn cried. "Cocooned in your luxury penthouse cushioned from all the hardships."

Eyes narrowed, Rafael asked, "Jealous, Kathryn? You had your chance. I sounded you out at Anna's party about being my wife. You weren't interested when you thought I was just the manager. Does owning the place make a difference to your view of me?"

Not a thousand hotels, she thought in anguish, only what I have in my heart — and not in yours! In great sadness she shook her head. "My answer is the same. Without love on both sides the marriage stands no chance."

"That settles it!" Picking up the holdall Rafael pounded up the steps and out of sight.

Sitting on the bottom tread Kathryn heard his car drive off and the silence once more overlay the beach. There was no breeze to dispel the sultriness or offer a respite from the heat clinging to the land. Too numb to cry Kathryn sat on while the sky darkened and the long evening died.

"Mum?" Deborah sat down on the same tread. "Are you all right?"

Kathryn put an arm round her. "I was watching the sea and thinking about home."

"It'll be nice to see our friends again," Deborah said. "We'll have a lot to tell them."

And so much we can't! Kathryn stood up and took Deborah's hand. Together they went up the steps, pausing for a look over the wide expanse of inky sea.

Deborah sat cross-legged on her bed in a flowered nightie. "I bet we'll have to write about our holidays when we get back to school. I'll have a lot to say."

"You always have!" Kathryn said in a weak attempt at a joke.

Deborah didn't respond. "Will we come back here one day?"

"I don't think so." Kathryn sat on the end of the bed. "We don't have that kind of money. It's sad to leave places you've grown to like, isn't it?"

"And people," Deborah added in a small voice.

"Yes," Kathryn agreed. "People, too."

Deborah bent her head. "I shall miss Anna and Rafael very much."

"Me, too." Kathryn's voice was as soft as Deborah's.

She helped her daughter into bed and kissed her good night then went for a shower. Kathryn got into bed and lay in the darkness for a while. Sleep deep enough to hold worry at bay came at last.

★ ★ ★

Kathryn woke with a start, jerking on to one elbow and listening. Someone was hammering on the outside door. She leapt from bed, pulled on a wrap and hurried through the living-room. In the kitchen, she halted by the rear door. The battering came again, shaking the wooden door and making the bolt rattle.

"Who's there?" she called, throat tight and nerves jumping.

"Kathryn? It's Rafael. Open the door."

"What do you want?" she demanded.

"I have to see you." The urgency of his tone reached through the door. "It won't wait. Open up!"

Kathryn took a pace away. "Come back in the morning."

"It is the morning," Rafael shouted. "Unbolt the door or I'll smash one of the windows!"

Muttering to herself Kathryn slid the bolt and turned the key, allowing the door to swing open. Rafael was in immediately, going through the kitchen and into the living-room without a word.

Incensed Kathryn shut the door and hastened after him. "What have you to say that's so important you have to get me from bed?"

"Nothing." His voice was calm for

all its tenseness. "I'm here to listen to you. I want an explanation of something you said on the beach last evening."

"You've got me up at this ungodly hour for that!" Kathryn could have stamped her foot in temper.

"For this I would have dragged you off the plane!"

Irritation began to give way to curiosity. Kathryn regarded his unsmiling features, unable to fathom what was behind the carefully controlled blankness.

She shrugged. "What's bothering you?"

"Remember we talked briefly about marriage!" The dark eyes were fixed on her face.

Kathryn's pulse jumped and she sat on the arm of a chair, one leg swinging in a would-be nonchalant way. "I believe we did."

"At Anna's party you said you wouldn't remarry unless you felt the same as the first time. Last night you said your answer was the same."

"So!" Kathryn had trouble sounding disinterested.

Very softly Rafael said, "But your answer wasn't the same, was it?"

His gaze held hers while Kathryn frantically attempted to recall the conversation on the beach. Rafael walked forward, pulled her upright and placed a hand on each side of her waist. "You said it needed love on *both* sides. That seems to show a change in your feelings." His hands moved up to hold her face so Kathryn couldn't look away. "Is that right?"

There was no way out nor did she search for one or consider lying. "Yes." The single word came firm and clear with no alteration of her expression.

Rafael expelled his breath in a long "Ahhh!" of what could have been relief or satisfaction, the hard features relaxing into a warm softness. His thumbs stroked gently across her cheeks in a way that created a whole new tangle in Kathryn's already disordered nerves. "You would have gone without saying a word and making us both unhappy," he chided.

Behind him Kathryn saw the fingers of dawn spike the darkness. The new day, her last in Spain, was being born. Sadness such as she'd never known settled around her, misting her eyes and sending a chill to every part. Her gaze came back to Rafael's face. "I'll get over it. Through the years I've learned to be resilient."

Gradually, as she stood silently in his arms, all the vitality drained from him. "Kathryn, what are you saying? You can't be turning your back on what we have, on what we could have!"

She felt the tremble in his hands against her skin and hardened her resolve. "Is this the moment to tell me you can't face the future without me and the rest of it." She forced his hands away. "Spare me that! I need no fair weather partner only one to trust and rely on." She walked to the window, arms wrapped round herself for comfort and warmth. "I'm every kind of idiot for loving you. I won't commit the folly of getting my life entangled with yours."

"What do you take me for!" He was across the room spinning Kathryn about to face his anger. "What is this nonsense?"

Weary to get the scene over Kathryn said, "I know all about Olivia."

The black brows snapped together. "I told you of her myself. The engagement was over years ago."

"I'm talking of now." Kathryn stared at the tanned throat showing at the open neck of his shirt then wished she hadn't. Love was a very physical emotion, eroding her will-power. "Maybe you consider you had cause to lead her on the way you did only to throw it back into her face. I wouldn't have believed it of you."

She couldn't look at him. In anguish Kathryn rocked backwards and forwards slightly, revealing with a sob, "Even now I would be prepared to take the risk with my happiness, but not with

Deborah's. Never with my daughter's!"

Her voice died away and the future with it. She waited for him to leave, knowing he wouldn't waste his time here any longer.

"I might have known Olivia has been stirring her witch's brew." Rafael was more exasperated than angry. "Tell me everything she said about the two of us.

His unexpected attitude caused a tiny flicker of hope to flare for Kathryn. He listened with unnerving attention and silence until her account was done.

"Clever Olivia!" His tone bordered upon the respectful. "She hit you just where you are most vulnerable — your knowledge of me or rather your lack of it."

"She was lying!" The hope grew a little stronger.

"No." The straight denial flattened Kathryn again. "She was too smart for that. She used the truth and you had no defence against it."

He remained close without touching

235

her. "I love you, Kathryn, and want to marry you. I can explain everything but I . . . "

"You really do love me?" Kathryn broke in, uncertainty and disbelief warring with the new-found hope.

"I really do!" His affirmation could not have been more clear or sincere.

Unbidden came his earlier declaration 'Olivia is not my lady-love'. She had believed it then yet had still allowed herself to be convinced otherwise. "Rafael, I'm sorry for not trusting you, for thinking you were capable of such behaviour."

For a moment they stared at one another, the truth shining between them. Both moving at the same instant, Kathryn was in his arms.

"Let's be sensible," Rafael said after a few minutes. "I want to tell you some things."

"Later." Kathryn was lost in the pure joy of this special time.

Rafael put a hand under her chin to lift her face up. "I don't want you to have any lingering doubts about my being the right man for your husband or as a father to Deborah." He led her to a chair, sitting opposite so he could see her clearly. "You know of my father's business collapse?"

"Francisca told me."

"My engagement broke up at the same time. I was quite shattered. Eventually I got myself together and the debts were settled. When Olivia's father offered me a job I refused at first but he persisted and in the end I agreed." He gave Kathryn a rueful smile. "I guess my working for him sounds odd to you but we'd always got on well and Olivia was away so there was nothing to disturb the arrangement. I never saw her until the funeral."

Rafael gazed ahead, thoughts locked deep in the past. "It was strange to meet the woman I'd been close to marrying and yet feel nothing. She could have been a chance acquaintance."

He got up and strolled over to unlock the terrace door to let in the early morning. The sun was up, painting the sky a pale blue, the air fresh and crisp. "Olivia's father left me four per cent of the Mediterraneo, the rest divided equally between Olivia and her son. There was also a condition that I could only sell to one of the other shareholders. Luis' share is held in trust and his trustee usually sides with me in matters affecting the hotel."

Kathryn came to stand beside him, an arm round his waist. Four per cent was a far smaller share than Olivia had implied.

Rafael dropped an arm across her shoulders. "Once the divorce was finalised Olivia came to live at the hotel. It didn't take long to realise Olivia believed I still felt the same about her. I had to get away before my position became intolerable. Early this year I heard the Christoval was up for sale."

"You actually are a hotel owner!" Kathryn could smile over it now.

"A small hotel owner," he confirmed.

"You've seen the place. It's hardly top class."

"You'll soon get it into the upper bracket."

"That is my intention," he grinned, "only my energies have been diverted these last few weeks."

"A good job I'm leaving today." Kathryn flicked him a look from under her lashes and got soundly kissed.

More seriously she asked. "Did your grandmother's money cover the hotel deal?"

"There was no large inheritance," Rafael corrected "just her life insurance amounting to a few thousand pounds. I invested it and added what I could from my salary. By living frugally I got a fair amount together but not enough to buy the Christoval. I had to sell the four per cent in the Mediterraneo."

He let go of Kathryn and went out on to the terrace, sat on the wall and rubbed a finger along its whitewashed surface. "While not exactly leading Olivia on, I didn't correct the construction she put on my wanting to sell. I told her it was for personal reasons and she made the wrong assumption."

Kathryn came to join him on the wall. "As an owner yourself, you'd have equal status with her and your masculine pride would be satisfied."

"Something like that." Rafael looked across to where the hotel could be seen over the rise of the land. "She agreed to buy my share at the end of the season. On the strength of that, together with this property, the bank advanced the money for the Christoval."

"Which is where I met you!"

"Yes, indeed," he chuckled. "What a little firebrand you were!"

"You didn't get scorched!" Kathryn teased.

"Not right away." There was a stirring in the dark eyes which made her flush slightly. "But later . . . "

Rafael jumped off the wall, taking Kathryn with him. "I need cooling down. Let's go for a swim."

The water hadn't had time to warm up and made Kathryn gasp. Rafael matched his strokes to hers in a lazy crawl that took them some fifty yards from the shore. "Deborah loves it here." Kathryn turned on her back and floated. "You won't go before she wakes, will you?"

"Certainly not." He headed for the beach with Kathryn in close pursuit. Reaching it first Rafael picked up a towel ready to drape it round her shoulders. He squinted upwards. "Don't want you burning."

Kathryn put an arm next to his. "See what a pale creature I am."

"A lovely sea nymph come to brighten my life."

"The Spanish charm's at work again!" Kathryn wiped her face. "Mind I don't swim off and not come back."

The teasing went from his expression. "I thought you really had gone the day Luis was so disobedient. Up until then you'd aroused my interest suffficiently for me to want you to stay longer. I arranged the change of tickets even before I asked you about it. Realising you could be drowning with Luis hit me like a thunderbolt." He touched her cheek. "Suddenly you were the most important person in my life. I was terrified it was too late."

He took the towel so he could rub his hair. "I came down that night only Deborah wouldn't let me in. I was worried sick about you. It was worse when Deborah told me you tried to leave." He handed back the towel.

"You won't get rid of me that easily." Kathryn dried her arms and legs. "What happened with Luis?"

"He's going to America with his father." Rafael scuffed at the sand with one foot. "Jorge Santini hadn't seen much of the boy since Olivia left. The custody of Luis was bitterly contested by both of them in the divorce court and Santini won. He came to get the boy and Olivia didn't want him to go."

"Poor Luis!" Kathryn's heart went

out to the six-year-old. "Why did you go rushing to Madrid?"

Rafael put his arm round her and they began walking towards the steps. "Because Olivia changed her mind over the deal. She refused to buy my four per cent."

Kathryn stopped. "It had been agreed! What about the bank loan?"

"Exactly!" Rafael's face mirrored his remembered anger. "Without the sale of my hotel share I couldn't have met the loan conditions. The bank would eventually have foreclosed and I'd have lost the Christoval as well as the house."

"Olivia was annoyed you'd taken us to Granada instead of her." Kathryn could see the chain of events. "Did this happen the night you were so upset?"

Rafael nodded. "When Olivia rang from Madrid I dashed off immediately." He smiled at her puzzled face. "I hadn't known Santini was over here for Luis. It was a long shot but it worked. He bought the four per cent on behalf of his son and put it into Luis' trust. As for the rest it was none of my business so I came back to you."

"What about us, Rafael?" Kathryn switched to their own problems. "I don't know how I'll bear leaving you."

"What we have is strong," Rafael reassured. "It will stand the separation and still grow."

Kathryn's answering smile was rather strained. "I keep thinking I'll wake up and be alone again."

Rafael's arms were a safe haven. "Only because love is so new. The distance makes no difference."

Kathryn put her arms round his neck. "I love you."

"I guessed you were not indifferent by the way you acted the other night on the beach. You were so mad." Rafael clasped his hands behind her back. "Then you accused me of playing around and wouldn't let me kiss you."

"You did anyway!" Kathryn reminded him.

"I'm sorry about that."

"I forgive you," she murmured, reaching up.

"Mum! Where are you?"

Kathryn raced for the steps. "I'm coming."

"I didn't know where you were," Deborah told her out-of-breath mother.

Rafael crouched in front of the little girl. "I'm coming to England to see you in February." He glanced at Kathryn. "I won't be able to get away before then."

"Will you stay with us?" Deborah was saucer-eyed with excitement. "You can have my room."

"We'll sort it out nearer the time," Kathryn said.

During breakfast Deborah kept up a flood of talk and questions, telling Rafael of all the things they could do when he came to visit.

"Don't think you're coming for a rest," Kathryn grinned, then shot out of her chair. "Look at the time! The taxi will be here in an hour."

"I cancelled it," Rafael revealed. "I'll take you to the airport."

It was quite a scurry round to get away on time, Anna kissing them both and waving furiously from the end of the drive. Rafael checked in their case then took them to the windows overlooking the runways so Deborah could watch the planes. He and Kathryn held hands and had difficulty speaking. The minutes ticked away and both knew the flight would soon be called.

"Phone to let me know you're home," Rafael said, "and write often. When I come in February we'll arrange about the summer. You and Deborah can stay at the house again."

"Thank you." Kathryn's throat closed up and she felt like crying.

"Don't start having doubts the moment we're apart. Everything has happened so quickly I feel in a complete whirl. I wish we'd had time to get a ring."

Kathryn managed a smile. "It doesn't

matter about a ring. I'll be taking your love with me."

"We'll get one together in February," Rafael said, "unless you want me to choose it."

"Yes, I would only . . ." she stopped, realising what she'd been about to say.

"You don't want one like your husband gave you."

"That hadn't occurred to me," Kathryn confessed. "To be honest I was going to say I didn't want the same as you gave to Olivia."

"No chance of that!" he denied instantly. "You're not the diamond solitaire sort. Much warmer and softer altogether."

Kathryn's brows came together. "I meant the one she showed me."

Rafael was nonplussed. "She couldn't have done! The ring was returned when the engagement was broken. I sold it and gave the money to charity."

"Well, Olivia said you'd given it to her."

"Wait," Rafael burst out. "Was it gold set with very small rubies?"

Kathryn nodded, holding on to the magic of their new love to face what he might say.

"I gave Olivia the ring as a birthday present before we became engaged. It was years ago." His face wore a worried expression. "You do believe me! It's hard to trust someone you've known for so short a time."

So the ring was at least ten years old, a fact carefully omitted by Olivia. Kathryn reached up to kiss his cheek. "Yes, with all my heart."

The flight announcement came over the loudspeaker and Kathryn looked at Rafael in sudden panic.

"I love you," he said softly. "Remember that when the uncertainties come."

At the top of the plane steps Kathryn looked back but couldn't see him. He's there, she said to herself, he always will be. Our love will grow and survive the partings until we can be together for good. High in the air she made plans.

Save what she could towards the flight ticket next year. Enroll for evening classes in Spanish.

"Would you like a drink?" The stewardess was smiling down at her. "Going home after a holiday? A bit sad when it ends." She handed over a cup and moved on.

Kathryn relaxed. Not an ending, she corrected. A beginning — to the rest of my life!

THE END